BUTTERFLY EFFECT

Ed Lazenby Mystery

CHARLES RAY

North Potomac, MD

This book is a work of fiction. Names, descriptions, places, and incidents are products of the author's imagination, or are used fictionally. Any resemblance to actual events or persons, living or dead, is purely coincidental.

For information about this and other works of this author, contact the author at charlesray.author@yahoo.com.

Cover photograph and cover design by the author.

Printed in the United States of America.

ISBN: 0692569790
ISBN-13: 978-0692569795

Dedication

To my students in the Osher Lifelong Learning Institute (OLLI) at Johns Hopkins University, who are the inspiration for this story.

ONE

"Pass the salt," the red-haired woman said. She stared across the table, a glint in her icy blue eyes, as if daring her dining companions to point out her lack of courtesy. Waiting for a response, she played with a bouncy tendril of hair that hung over her left ear.

Ed Lazenby ran a medium brown left hand slowly through his close-cropped black hair, almost able to feel the gray that streaked through the waves that resulted from the vigorous brushing he'd given it that morning. His expression was neutral. He was accustomed to Violet Wertheim's bluntness and lack of manners, so he ignored her, looking instead at the pork chops and home fried potatoes on his plate.

Their two dining companions, Violet's sister, Rose, and Ed's best friend, Ernesto Cardoza, sat in quiet tension, waiting for Ed to point out Violet's failure to use the magic word 'please,' which would be required before he passed her the salt which was near his right hand, and too far away for her to reach. Neither of them would even dare reach across Ed to do it. He was known to be adamant on such things. No courtesy, no service.

Moments passed. Everyone maintained stony expressions, except Violet, whose cheeks bloomed pink against her pale face. She tapped one of her long, bright red fingernails against the bowl of soup in front of her, making a clicking sound.

"It would really be nice if I could get the salt," she said. There was a tinge of stridency in her voice.

Ed looked across the table at her, following up with a stoic gaze at Rose on his right, and then Ernesto on his left. Violet returned his gaze with a semi-glare, but the other two found the bowls of soup sitting in front of them more interesting. It had been that way for the three years he'd been a resident of Potomac Valley Community, a collection of small cottages and apartment units for people aged 65 and over, known as PVC to all the residents. Located on the east side of Norbeck Road, four miles north of Georgia Avenue, it was one of several retirement communities in the area. While most people just called it PVC because of the tendency in the Washington, DC area to reduce everything to initials, many of the residents, Ed included, likened it to the sewer pipes made of the same material. The houses were small, but had more space than the condos, and he liked having a lawn. Laid out in a grid pattern with interconnecting winding paths, the streets had names like Wisteria, Cypress, Palm, and Maple. Most of the trees on the main part of the grounds, though, were oak and birch, with a few evergreens. There was also an 18-hole golf course, six tennis courts, shuffle board courts, and several small buildings used for art lessons, pottery, and several other activities that residents were encouraged to participate in. Across Norbeck was a row of small, modest single story homes owned by people who'd lived in the area long before the retirement communities went up, and behind PVC was a large, undeveloped forest park where deer, squirrels, and other wildlife romped in profusion, since no hunting was allowed in the vicinity of the community.

He'd moved there two days after his birthday, a day after his retirement from his job as a systems analyst for the Department of Defense. He'd met, Ernesto, a retired postal worker, the first day. Like him, Ernesto was 68, and, both being widowers, had hit it off immediately. The Wertheim sisters, Violet, age 70, and Rose, age 66, had been a part of their foursome for only eighteen months, and despite the continual standoff between Ed and Violet over courtesy, they were the closest of friends. Violet and Rose had never been married, a fact that Ed had concluded was what led to Violet's abrasive personality. He could never figure out why the younger Wertheim sister was so sweet natured—probably a defense mechanism to enable her to get along with her more abrasive older sibling. When Violet got off on one of her tirades, usually having to do with the poor quality of the food served in the dining room of PVC's large community center, Rose would just play with her short hair, which on this particular evening had been dyed bright blue.

Finally, as he'd known would happen, he took a deep breath and focused his brown eyes on Violet.

"You know, Vi," he said, making an effort to keep the frustration he felt out of his voice. "It would be nice if you'd say please once in a while."

Violet made a snorting sound, which was easy to do given her large nose that to Ed resembled a pink banana that had been cut off near the end. That was another difference between the sisters. Rose's nose was small and narrow, straight from bridge to the end.

"Aw, give it a rest, Ed," she said. "What's such a big deal about one little word? You'd think the world will come to an end if I don't say please when I ask you to do something."

"Well now, Violet my dear, it might seem a small thing to you, but to the person on the receiving end, it just might be the biggest thing to happen to him or her all day." He paused and looked at her, his left eyebrow arched. "Now, do you still want that salt?"

She rolled her eyes. "Small things, small

things; I'll bet you're one of those people who believe a butterfly flapping its wings in the Amazon can cause a hurricane in Texas."

Ed shrugged.

"I don't know about that," he said. "But, I do know that a small change in one state of a deterministic nonlinear system can result in large differences in a later state. That's a part of chaos theory. It's like when you throw dice. Small changes in the trajectory, the force exerted, the angle at which you hold your hand, can have an impact on what numbers turn up. That's why it's impossible to throw dice twice exactly the same way. Edward Lorenz came up with the name butterfly theory for the phenomenon, although when he first studied it, the example was a seagull flapping its wings."

Violet rolled her eyes and snorted again.

"Do you really believe that crap? I mean, seriously, a seagull's wings?"

"I'm no meteorologist, so I don't know diddly about the weather or birds either for that matter. But, when I did systems analysis at the Defense Department, I saw for myself how tiny little maladjustments could sometimes screw up an entire system. Like a GI failing to make sure a key screw on a tank tread was properly tightened, causing the tread to loosen during a maneuver, throwing off a whole plan because a key tank couldn't get where it was needed, when it was needed. So, yeah, Vi, I do believe that crap. It's for real."

Ernesto slapped his brown hand on the

table, causing the dishes to rattle.

"That's for sure," he said. "When I was delivering mail one time, I stopped for a little mid-morning snack. Bought myself a hot dog, but didn't have time to eat it all, so I rolled it up in the napkin and put it on the dash of my mail van. I'd plumb forgot about it until about an hour later, I was just about to get out and put mail in this apartment's mailboxes, when this big damn Doberman came roaring out of a vacant lot beside the building." He paused and took a sip of soup, smacking in satisfaction. "Anyway, there I was, my hands full of mail and the door wide open, and this big dog coming at me full tilt. I backed up into the van, and as I was doing so, I accidentally knocked that damned leftover hotdog out onto the sidewalk. Dog screeched to a full stop and ignored me as he wolfed that hotdog down. Gave me time to get in the van and close the door and get the hell out of there."

Rose Wertheim bobbed her head up and down. Her blue-dyed hair cut short, hanging just over the tops of her ears waving with the motion.

"I agree. You remember, Violet, that time you found Uncle Mortimer's spectacles for him. Just a small thing, but he was so impressed, when he died, he left everything to you."

Violet laid a bony finger against the side of her prominent nose, smiling wistfully. With her free hand she caught the end of one of her scarlet curls and twisted it.

"Yes, I do remember that," she said. "It was the only thing I ever did for the old coot, but he thought it was the nicest thing anyone had ever done for him. Truth is, it probably was." She looked at Ed and then Ernesto. "You have to understand . . . our Uncle Mortimer was a real turd."

"Violet, watch your language. Ladies don't talk like that," Rose said.

"Oh, pshaw, Rose, stop being such a goody two shoes."

Rose's cheeks reddened.

"I am *not* a goody two shoes," she protested. "I just don't believe in using filthy language."

"Why is it you never say anything to Ed or Ernesto? These two reprobates curse like sailors sometimes."

Rose's cheeks got darker, and she looked at Ernesto from beneath lowered lids.

"Oh, they don't curse all that much," she said. "Besides, it's different for men."

Violet laughed a hoarse, deep throated laugh that caused Ed to cringe—hopefully not so much that she'd notice.

"Rose, darling," she said. "If it's okay for a man to say something, it should be okay for a woman, or have you decided to turn in your women's lib pin?"

"Of course not . . . it's just . . . oh, never mind, go ahead and be as foul-mouthed as you want to be."

Janet Murphy, a short blonde with small breasts and wide hips, wearing a pair of brown pants that reached to the middle of her thin calves but stretched across her hips, had been standing nearby watching the four old friends banter. With a smile on her pixie-like face she walked up to the table, standing behind Violet.

"Aren't you guys going to finish your soup, so you can try the special main course I've prepared for tonight?"

Murphy was the dietician for PVC. She had been for eight years. A thirty-one year old native of nearby Rockville, Maryland, she'd started out as an assistant to the dietician, taking over the job two years later, upon her boss's retirement. While her cooking sometimes left something to be desired, it was at least palatable most of the time, and Ed liked the fact that she always had a smile on her face, and she was unfailingly polite to everyone.

"What is tonight's special, Janet?" Ed asked.

"We're having surf and turf," she said. "I received a shipment of lobsters, and am serving them with filet mignon and baby carrots."

"I hope the steak's tender this time," Violet said. "Last time, I almost broke a tooth trying to chew it."

Murphy's face flushed dark crimson, her mouth opening and closing, and tears welling up in the corner of her eyes. She fiddled with the top button of her white blouse.

"Violet Anne Wertheim," Rose said. "You should be ashamed of yourself. You're making this sweet young thing cry."

"Yeah, Violet," Ernesto said, laying a hand

on Rose's arm as he spoke, causing her cheeks to go red. "That's not nice, not nice at all."

Violet shot Ed an imploring look, her brows raised.

"What they said," he said simply. Not that he disagreed with her. The steaks in question had been so tough; he'd taken so long to eat even half of one; he'd passed on dessert.

Violet shrugged and pursed her lips, looking like a student who's just been chastised by the principal.

"Oh, all right." She turned and looked up at Murphy. "I'm sorry, dear. I was just being cranky, you know. Comes with being old, I guess. The steak was really unique, and I'm sure tonight's steak will be just the same."

There wasn't an iota of sincerity in her voice, and Ed noticed that she hadn't said the steak tasted good. But, Janet Murphy didn't seem to notice, or if she did, didn't seem to care. She beamed proudly.

"Why thank you, Violet," she said. "I'll prepare a plate especially for you . . . some extra carrots, and you get an extra helping of dessert. We're having chocolate mousse tonight."

"You can keep the extra carrots, dear, but I do like the idea of an extra helping of dessert."

Murphy was still smiling when she turned away.

"Hey, Violet," Ed said. "Your soup's getting cold."

"But, it's not salty enough," she said.

Ed cocked his head to one side and looked down at the salt shaker.

"Oh, all right," she said, blowing a gust of air through her lips. "Ed, would you pass the salt, please?"

He picked the shaker up and bowed his head as he passed it across to her.

"Most happy to oblige, my dear," he said. "Now, that wasn't so bad was it?"

She ignored him for a few seconds as she sprinkled an unhealthy amount of salt into her soup. Then she dipped her spoon into the cream of spinach soup and stirred until the layer of salt crystals floating on the surface was pulled under. She filled the spoon and made slurping noises as she ate it.

"Hmm, now that's good." She looked at Ed. "It was . . . oh, how can I put this? It was at least better than getting a colonoscopy."

TWO

The steak actually turned out to be edible—a bit tough, but edible—and the lobster was, in Violet's words, divine, which coming from her was high praise. She passed on the carrots, and had a second helping of dessert. The four of them had coffee after dinner, played a few hands of bridge, and then retired to their separate residences, three small cottages in the same block of Wisteria Lane, after agreeing to meet the following day, Saturday at 7:30, for brunch and coffee in the community's center.

As friends often tend to do, the four of them shared common tastes, often selecting, without consultation, the same dishes when they dined together. This Saturday was no different. They each took scrambled eggs, ham, toast, coffee, and orange juice. After the first forkful of scrambled eggs, Violet made a face as if she'd just bitten into an unripe persimmon.

"Oh, my goodness," she said. "Eating these eggs is like chewing on cotton wool."

Ed looked around. Janet Murphy stood near

the heavily laden buffet table, smiling over each resident who passed by. He was concerned that she might hear Violet's critique. Not that it was unjustified—his first mouthful of eggs was like biting down on cardboard—but, he felt that Murphy tried her best, and it wasn't fair to constantly pick at her over her shortcomings. It would be nice if PVC had a cook who could actually . . . cook, but he wasn't sure there was anything the residents could do about other than cook their own meals—something he avoided as often as possible. What Ed did know was that if encouraged, Violet could go on for hours, and the more she talked, the more strident and insulting she often became. Even though he had to wash each forkful down with a large swallow of either coffee or orange juice, he soldiered on, ignoring Violet's outburst. Rose and Ernesto were accustomed to following Ed's lead. Neither of them relished being on the receiving end of Violet's outbursts, so they just shoved the scrambled eggs aside and focused on the other items on their plates.

Violet wasn't stupid. She knew when she was being willfully ignored.

"*Well*, am I right or not? Are these not the absolute worse eggs you're ever eaten."

She was getting louder. Ed wanted to divert her; in the first instance to spare Murphy's feelings, and in the second, because he and Ernesto had a round of golf scheduled for immediately after the meal and he didn't want the mental distraction screwing up his already way-too-much over par game.

"Actually, Violet," he said quietly. "They're *not* the worse, not by a long shot. When I was in the army, we sometimes got powdered eggs in the mess hall."

In that he was telling the truth. In some of the facilities he'd been forced to eat in in the army, the food was horrible. Murphy couldn't seem to get eggs right unless she boiled them. He recalled the scrambled eggs from Sunday brunch a few weeks earlier—they'd been undercooked. The sight of slimy egg white floating next to his bacon had almost undone him. Violet's eyes went wide. She too remembered.

"Oh, you're right," she said. "In that case, I guess you're right, and I'm wrong."

She looked at Ed, her brows still raised, waiting for him to say something. Ed turned his attention back to his plate, eating around the offending eggs. Finally, when it was clear that no one would rise to her baiting, Violet did the same.

After putting away the meal—albeit with some effort—they lingered a bit longer over coffee. The coffee, they all agreed, was the only thing Murphy did well, extremely well.

Ed looked across the table at Violet. An attractive woman, despite her sour disposition; what some would call well preserved. As long as she was occupied with something positive and pleasant, she wasn't too bad to be around. Ed desperately wanted to keep the morning on a positive track.

"Violet," he said. "Last night you were telling us about your Uncle Mortimer. Sounds like an interesting character."

Since the old guy was long since dead, it seemed a safe subject. Violet bit.

"Uncle Mortimer . . . what a pill . . . daddy used to say that Uncle Mortimer was a waste of good air. They were brothers, but they never got along." Her face took on a wistful expression. "He hated everything and everyone. Never had a good word to say about a living soul."

Like someone else we all know, Ed thought, but kept his expression blank.

"He couldn't have been all that bad," Ed said. "After all, he did leave you his entire fortune. He must have liked you."

"I don't think it was so much that he liked me as it was he hated everyone else. And, don't forget, I was the one who found his eyeglasses for him. Everyone else would sit around and giggle behind their hands when he misplaced things. I guess he thought I was salvageable."

Ed had a sense that Violet wasn't telling the whole story of her relationship with her uncle, which was a bit of a problem. He was a man who couldn't resist a puzzle, and her story was just too cryptic—too pat. He had a hard time getting his mind around a man passing all of his relatives by in his will and leaving everything to one who had only found his eyeglasses for him.

"You sure you didn't do other nice things for

your uncle . . . things that you've maybe forgotten?"

She scrunched up her forehead and pursed her lips.

"Well . . . let me think . . . no I'm pretty sure that's the only nice thing I ever did for him."

Her eyes darted away when she spoke. Ed knew immediately that she'd lied to him. The question that would nag at him until he found an answer was, why? He'd never known her to lie to him before in all the time they'd known each other. What was it about her uncle that motivated her to seek shelter in lies? He *would* find out. But, he'd have to be discrete—another word for sneaky—and approach the problem indirectly.

"You know, I think you really liked your uncle," he said.

Violet leaned back in her chair, regarding Ed down the length of her nose—a long way to look over her oversized schnozz.

"I am nothing like my uncle," she said with a dose of indignation that had to rate in the high megaton range.

"I didn't say-" Then Ed cut himself off. Violet was a lot of things, but hard of hearing was *not* one of them. He knew very well that she'd heard him clearly. Why had she chosen to respond the way she did? He smiled. This was going to be interesting. "Never mind," he said. "I was just guessing. Can't always be right."

Violet acted like she hadn't heard him. "Well, I suppose I do believe some of the same things he believed. Doesn't make me like him, mind you, because some of his beliefs made perfect sense. For instance, he always used to say, don't try to make omelets if you're not willing to break a few eggs. Now, that makes perfect sense, don't you think."

"I suppose it does." Ed had no idea where that had come from. Rose and Ernesto, who had been silently following the conversation looked like spectators at a tennis match as their heads swiveled from side to side, watching the two gladiators go at it. Ernesto finally broke the mood, by tapping his plate with his fork, causing all eyes to turn to him.

"Hey, amigo," he said. "We have an 8:24 tee time. Don't want to be late."

Golf was one of Ed's passions. He didn't consider himself a good golfer, but he enjoyed testing himself against the course and during a round, he had time to think about other things. He got some of his best ideas while trying to blast out of a greenside bunker—usually unsuccessfully. In fact, the quality of his ideas was often in direct opposition to the quality of his game.

"Okay, compadre, let's get a move on. Our clubs are already at the starter shack." He'd taken them there as soon as he woke up, so they wouldn't have to waste time going back to their homes after brunch.

The path from the community center to the first green of the community's private golf course wound between two six-story condos and transited a street lined on both sides with the little bungalows for those who didn't like apartment living. The houses were small, one-story cottages, in deference to the age of their occupants. No stairs to negotiate. They were identical, with a living room off the main entrance, kitchen and dining room off to the right, and two identically sized bedrooms to the left. Front and back yards were the only means residents had of expressing their individuality. Ed and Ernesto hadn't done anything to the landscaping that was there when they purchased, so their houses were identical, inside and out, and were located across the street from each other. The Wertheim sisters owned a cottage three buildings down from Ed and Ernesto, but had gone hog wild with a profusion of flowers—perennials and annuals—and shrubbery, giving their cottage the appearance of an English country estate, albeit a tiny one.

They arrived at the starter shack at 8:20, to deep frowns from the starter, a rotund man with a Santa Claus beard and a totally bald head named Brian—Ed could never remember his last name. Golfers were asked to arrive 10 minutes prior to tee time. Four minutes was . . . in his words, rude. But, he happened to like Ed and Ernesto, knew they played a fairly fast game, and wouldn't delay foursomes behind them, so he just snorted and gave them their score cards, stubby pencils, and a key to their cart.

The four Koreans who were scheduled to tee off behind them, though, were incensed. They muttered loudly in Korean, glaring at Ed and Ernesto. Ed had nothing against the Korean residents of the community, though he did wonder why they would want to live in such a place since they hardly ever socialized with the non-Korean residents. Where he found them hard to take, though, was on the golf course, where they talked loud, took their sweet time when you were playing behind them, but insisted that you play at warp speed when they were behind you. He didn't ever recall seeing one of them smile on the course. He dealt with them, though, by ignoring them.

Ernesto on the other hand found their rude behavior intolerable, and couldn't resist responding to their activity.

"Hey, guys," he said. "What's the problem? You don't want to play behind us or something?"

"You come late," one of the men, a short, squat man with jet black hair—from the sheen, from a bottle—and bowlegs. "You should let us go first."

Ernesto walked over and stood in front of the man. He had to bend to be nose to nose.

"Well now, amigo, that ain't gonna happen," he said. "I promise you, we'll play fast—faster than you dudes do with your betting and such. So, just chill your jets."

The man looked confused. He turned and said something in harsh, rapid fire Korean. Ed and Ernesto got in their cart and with Ed driving went to the first tee.

Ernesto leaned out and looked back at the Koreans who were walking behind them, still engaged in an animated conversation.

"Hey, guys," he said. "I better tell you; I'm a postal worker—retired—but, if you keep making that noise behind us, I just might go postal on you."

The four men stopped and stared open mouthed at Ernesto. For all of their pretense of not understanding or speaking good English, they got the significance of 'going postal.'

"You know, Ernesto," Ed said. "One of these days they're gonna call your bluff."

"Well, if they do, I'll just have to go postal, now won't I?" The two men chuckled. "Say, whaddya think about Violet's story about her uncle?"

"What do you mean, what do I think?"

"She got kind of evasive there when you started talking about their relationship."

"You caught that too? I don't know. There's something there she doesn't want to talk about."

"So, you're gonna find out what it is."

It wasn't a question. Ernesto had come to know Ed well, as Ed did him. Ed wasn't surprised that his friend had caught the same vibes he had.

"I'm gonna try," he said. "Now, let's play golf."

They did 'rock, paper, scissors,' to see who

would tee off first. Ernesto had scissors, Ed had rock. He laughed.

After hitting his first shot, he stopped laughing. His ball was long, around 280 yards, but was a good ten feet into the long rough on the right.

"You need to work on that slice, amigo," Ernesto said.

"Shut up and hit your ball."

Ernesto went through his pre-shot routine, which involved wiggling his hips and taking several deep breaths. His swing was more like an attempt to behead the ball than a golf swing, but he beat Ed's distance by a good ten yards— in the left rough.

It went that way for the first eight holes. On nine, both of them finally found the fairway, but only by sacrificing more than sixty yards driving distance. Ed got his first par on twelve, which he took as a good omen, because the tee box for thirteen was on a hill overlooking a small valley containing a small natural pond that was a favorite stopping place for water fowl. An avid bird watcher since his teens, Ed liked to stand on the hill overlooking the pond to see what species he could identify.

Because the little dip in the land was out of play from errant balls from anywhere on the course, it was also where Louis Palmer, the groundskeeper and maintenance man had constructed his storage shed. The building's proximity to the pond, Ed noticed thankfully, didn't seem to bother the many birds that congregated on its shores. Nor did the presence of Palmer, who Ed saw rolling a gas powered mulcher into the shed.

As they stepped up to the thirteenth tee, Ed let Ernesto and his lengthy pre-shot routine go first, even though his birdie entitled him. While Ernesto did his butt wiggling, Ed walked to the end of the tee box and gazed down at the pond. To his delight, a pair of great blue herons stood in the shallow water at the pond's edge. From the 'awk, awk, awk,' sound they made, and the way they kept clacking their beaks together, he figured them for a nesting pair. Just as he turned to prepare to take his shot, a flock of Canada geese swooped in, honking loudly as they splashed into the middle of the pond. The herons continued to make their courting sounds, ignoring the raucous geese. Ed smiled broadly. *Nice how nature lets creatures coexist.*

On thirteen he hit the ball down the middle of the fairway a scorching two hundred ninety yards, made the green in two and one-putted. *Who said thirteen was an unlucky number?*

-

THREE

Golf ended as it usually did; Ernesto was ahead so many strokes by hole thirteen that Ed decided to quit keeping score. On their way back to the clubhouse to turn in the cart, they noticed the Korean foursome just teeing off on ten. Ernesto could resist waving at them. They refused to look back.

"Hey, leave 'em alone," Ed said.

Ernesto shrugged. "Sorry, I can't help it. They're so self- righteous, and never, I mean never, admit when they make a mistake."

"Yeah, well, you shouldn't let it get to you. What do you want to do for lunch?"

Violet and Rose invited us to a late lunch at their place, don't you remember?"

After parking their cart, they took their clubs for the trek along the path between the condos to Wisteria Lane. They took both sets of clubs to Ed's house.

They had a standing bet; loser cleaned the winner's clubs; and even though they'd stopped keeping score, Ed conceded that Ernesto would have won. In fact, in their years of playing together, Ed had only twice *not* been the one to clean the clubs.

"Okay, I'm taking a shower and changing," Ed said after they stacked the clubs against the wall on the patio. "I'll come over in about thirty minutes and we can walk down to Rose and Violet's place."

After Ernesto left, Ed went to his garage, where he kept his old silver Toyota 4-Runner, and got a bucket, a scrub brush and an old bathroom towel from a rack beneath the tool bench. He filled the bucket from the faucet at the back of his house and began scrubbing the clubs, starting with the irons. After removing dirt and grass particles from the club faces and hozzles, he rubbed them dry with the towel. He then repeated the same process with the woods, taking particular care with the drivers.

The clubs were stacked in two groups, in order from driver to putter, next to the golf bags. Leaving them to dry in the sun, he carefully wiped off his golf shoes and draped the towel over the back of a wicker chair, and then, after dumping the dirty water around the roots of the azalea bush at the corner of his patio, took the bucket and brush back to the garage.

He went inside and to the bathroom where he removed his golf shoes and clothing, at first dumping everything on the floor in an untidy pile, but as he dumped his underwear, he heard his late wife's voice in his mind. *Edward Lazenby, don't you be leaving your dirty clothes piled on the floor like that. That's what we have laundry hampers for.* He felt a burning in his eyes, unshed tears, even as he smiled. Victoria had been like that—a place for everything, and everything in its place. He chuckled. She always nagged him about tidiness, which annoyed him at the time, but he really missed it now that she was gone. The memories came back at the oddest times and places, and even after five years, he still missed her. Sometimes, he resented the fact that ovarian cancer had stolen her chance to enjoy retirement with him.

He shook it off. *The past is something that can't be undone.* Something else she'd often say whenever he bemoaned some missed opportunity. He turned on the water, as hot as he could stand, and stood underneath the shower, letting the hot water cascade over him.

Shower finished, he toweled off, shaved, and brushed his hair until it had just the right amount of wave. He then dressed in a pair of tan slacks and a powder blue polo shirt, topping that off with tan socks and a pair of brown leather loafers, buffed to a mirror-like shine. He checked the time as he slipped his Bulova watch onto his right wrist—fifteen minutes until the lunch with the Wertheim sisters.

He walked across the street to Ernesto's house. His friend opened the door just as he was reaching for the buzzer.

"Hey, bro," Ernesto said. "You clean up nice."

The one thing Ed could always count on was Ernesto ribbing him about the way he dressed. He stood there in his doorway, wearing a pair of khaki cargo pants that ended mid-calf, with a puke green long sleeved shirt that looked as if it had been taken directly from the dryer with no ironing to remove the wrinkles, outside the pants. Sockless, on his size twelve feet he had pink flip flops. It was warm for October, so light dress was appropriate, but Ernesto looked like he had just returned from a scavenger hunt through the Montgomery County landfill.

"Ernie, my boy," Ed said. "I wish I could say the same for you."

Ernesto looked down at his feet. He lifted the edge of his shirt with his pudgy fingers.

"What's wrong with what I'm wearing?"

"Nothing if you're going dumpster diving."

"Hey, it's just lunch with Violet and Rose, man. It's not like we're going to some fancy afternoon tea."

Ed knew, though, that with the Wertheim's, especially Violet, it *was* likely to be just that. Even though they'd been born and raised in Rockville, Maryland, and had never been south of Richmond, Virginia in their lives, she had what amounted to an obsession with the plantation society of the antebellum south. She was likely to be wearing a dress with plenty of wide petticoats and a scooped neckline. Rose, accustomed to living in her older sister's shadow, would be similarly dressed. If the two of them had been the fussy type, he would be considered underdressed, but thankfully, Rose never fussed about anything, and Violet never paid much attention to what other people wore, so they would accept him. Ernesto they would also accept, because he was . . . Ernesto. Even though he was always threatening to 'go postal,' he was such an outgoing, friendly, bear of a man, everyone liked him. Ed suspected that Rose actually had something of a romantic thing for him.

"Well, if you feel comfortable, I guess that's the only thing that matters," he said. "We still have almost fifteen minutes, and you know Violet and Rose never start anything on time. It's only a three minute walk to their house, so what'll we do to kill time."

"I think I hear a hint in there somewhere. You wouldn't be suggesting a little before lunch sip, would you, maybe a touch of bourbon on the rocks?"

"Why, Ernesto Cardozo, I do believe you're a mind reader."

"Nah, just an old postman who learned to know what people wanted . . . come on in."

He stepped aside and let Ed enter, then followed him into the living room. Ed flopped down on the sofa while Ernesto poured two fingers of amber liquid from a square bottle with a black label into two water glasses.

"Jim Beam Black," Ed said. "You're moving up in the world."

"You gonna drink, drink the best. None of that rotgut passing itself off as whiskey for me."

Ed chuckled as he took a sip. It was good whiskey. *If he only had the same taste in clothes.* But, hey, it didn't matter. Friends didn't obsess over such trivialities as clothing—especially friends who were getting as long in the tooth as the two of them were. It wasn't as if either of them had to dress to impress the ladies any longer. He looked at his watch.

"Shouldn't we be going?"

Ernesto drained the last of his drink and reached for the bottle.

"Hell, we have time for one more . . . don't you think?"

Ed looked at his glass. He had about a finger of liquor left. *Damn, I didn't even notice drinking it. It is smooth, though. Oh, what the hell.* He drained the glass and held it out to allow Ernesto to pour in another two fingers.

"You want ice?" Ernesto asked.

Ed sniffed. The woody odor warmed his nose.

"No, I'll just do this one neat." He took a sip and sighed.

"Yeah, no point spoiling good bourbon with ice," Ernesto agreed and took a sip as well.

They finished the second drinks in companionable silence. After draining his glass, Ed put his glass on the coffee table, which was covered with rings from previous drinking sessions.

"Well, I think we should get going," he said. "We'll be fashionably late; I don't want to be sloshed along with it."

Ernesto frowned. He looked longingly at his

glass. Then, he sighed and drained it, and placed it next to Ed's on the table.

"Yeah, I guess you're right."

He teetered slightly as he stood, but after taking a deep breath, steadied himself.

By the time they were outside, and Ernesto was locking his door, he was rock steady. Ed marveled at the man's ability to metabolize alcohol. He was still a bit unsteady himself, and was sure Violet would give them grief as soon as she smelled the booze on their breath. He cursed himself for forgetting to put breath mints in his pocket, and then shrugged. He remembered the old joke he'd heard in the army, 'what do you get when you spray air freshener in an elevator after someone farts? The smell of a fart in a pine forest.' The mints would only add itself to the whiskey smell. He would just have to endure Violet's nagging.

The brisk air helped clear his head, so that by the time they arrived at the Wertheim's house, the effects of the whiskey on Ed had mostly worn off. He rang the bell. When the door swung inward, he turned his head to minimize the possibility of his whiskey breath giving him away too soon.

Rose Wertheim, wearing a yellow frock that stopped just below her knees, stood in the door. Instead of her usual smile, she wore a worried look. She stepped aside and allowed Ed and Ernesto to enter the living room. As he passed her, Ed noticed that she didn't make eye contact. In fact, she hadn't greeted them as she usually did.

"Rose," he asked. "Is something wrong?"

Her eyes darted to her left.

"Uh, well . . . I . . . why don't you two come on in and have a seat."

When Ed followed her gaze, he saw that there was another person present, and that it wasn't her sister Violet. It took Ed a few seconds to recognize Peony Lake, the only daughter of Violet and Rose's younger sister, Daisy. Daisy, Ed had been told, had died in an auto accident when Peony was thirteen, and she'd lived with her two aunts until she graduated high school and went off to college. Now thirty, she worked as a graphics designer in New York, and only came to visit her aunts on holidays. Unlike her aunts, though, she was not into formal dress. If anything, with her faded blue jeans, cut outs showing her bony knees, and a wrinkled New York Mets sweatshirt, she looked more like Ernesto's relative or drinking buddy, than a Wertheim. Her dark brown hair was cropped close to her narrow skull. She sat on the couch, clutching a glass of red wine in her right hand and a wrinkled sheet of paper in her left.

Warning signals went off in Ed's head. Rose's nervousness and Peony's presence—and, Violet's absence—something was wrong.

He turned on Rose. "Okay, Rose, I know something's wrong. Where's Violet? What's going on?"

Peony put her wineglass down and stood.

"Hello, Mr. Lazenby," she said as she walked toward him. "It's been a while." She extended a slender hand.

Ed shook her hand. Her grip was firm and dry. "Hi, Peony, nice to see you, too, although I didn't expect you to visit until Thanksgiving."

"Uh, yeah. I came down to visit Aunt Rose and Aunt Vi to discuss a personal problem I'm having."

Ernesto came up behind Ed.

"Having man problems, Peony?" he asked.

Her cheeks flamed red, and she glared at him.

"Cut the kid some slack, Ernesto," Ed said to defuse the tension. "Besides, there's something else wrong. I can feel it. right, ladies?"

Peony laughed. "I see Aunt Vi was right about you."

"Right about me what?" Ed's left brow rose.

"She said you were very perceptive; that nothing got past you. You're right, there is another problem, one we need your help on."

"What kind of problem?"

"Aunt Violet's been kidnapped," she said. She handed him the paper.

FOUR

After handing Ed the paper, Peony put her arms around her aunt's shoulder and led her to the couch where they both sat; Rose looking confused and Peony looking stone faced. Ed couldn't help notice that, sitting so close together, the two women looked more like sisters than Rose and Violet looked when they were together. He then looked down at the paper Peony had handed him.

It was a simple sheet of 8 by 10-inch bond paper—the kind you can buy by the ream in any CVS or Office Depot—covered with letters and words that, from the glossy paper, had been cut from magazines. The fragments had been glued to the paper in precise lines, centered on the sheet.

WE HAVE TAKEN VIOLET
DO NOT CALL THE POLICE
OR WE WILL KILL HER
WE WILL CONTACT YOU
LATER WITH OUR DEMANDS

"Holy shit," Ernesto said. He'd been peering over Ed's shoulder. "We gotta call the cops."

"No!" Rose and Peony spoke as one. Peony rose from the sofa.

"You read it. If we call the police, they'll kill her," she said.

Ed shook his head. He ran a hand over his head.

"She's right, Ernesto," he said. "We can't take a chance like that with Violet's life."

"Okay, okay, I guess you're right, but what are we gonna do?"

Ed looked over at the two women.

"First, I want you two to tell us what happened. Who gave you the note?"

Rose and Peony looked at each other. The younger woman then looked at Ed. "It was on the coffee table when Aunt Rose and I got back from the grocery store," she said, clearly taking charge.

"So, Violet was here alone," Ed said. "How long?"

"Oh, I don't know . . . thirty minutes, maybe an hour. Do you remember, Aunt Rose?"

Rose shook her head. She kept her gaze focused on the coffee table.

"I-I . . . I suppose so . . . an hour sounds . . . right."

"And when we got back, we came from the garage to the kitchen through the back door," Peony said. "We called to let Aunt Vi know we were back, and received no answer, so we looked for her in the bedroom, but she wasn't there either."

Ed looked around the room. He tried to picture in his head the two women entering the kitchen and calling out for Violet.

"What did you do then?"

"We came in here. Aunt Rose noticed the paper on the coffee table. That's it."

"When did all this happen?" Ed asked.

"I don't know, maybe twenty minutes ago . . . or less," she said. "Just before the two of you came."

"Who do you think is doing this?" Ernesto asked.

Rose shook her head again. "I don't know," she said. "We don't know hardly any people outside the community except Peony. She's just about the only relative we have left."

"What are we going to do?" Peony asked, looking directly at Ed.

Ed sighed. Responsibility for managing this mess was being thrust upon him, a responsibility he didn't want, but he saw no way to avoid it.

"For now, there's not much we can do but wait," he said. "We'll see what the kidnapper's next demands are, and then decide. In the meantime, I want you to walk me through the morning in as much detail as you can; everything you remember."

"Why?" Rose asked in a querulous voice. "How will that help get Violet back?"

"I don't know, but the more information I

have the better I'll be able to come up with some kind of plan. Besides, sometimes it's the seemingly insignificant details that can be the most important, so humor me."

"He's probably right, Aunt Rose," Peony said. Ed felt grateful for her rational response.

"So, maybe Ernesto and I can take you two ladies out for lunch," he said. "There's a Pizza place down on Georgia Avenue. We can talk while we eat."

"We were planning to eat here," Rose said. "I made a nice Caesar salad and tuna sandwiches."

"Sure, if that's what you want," Ed said. "I just figured you'd rather not be bothered with cooking. I suppose it is a better idea, though. We need to be here for the kidnapper's next note."

He was still having trouble getting his mind around the idea of someone kidnapping Violet Wertheim. Other than her comments about her uncle leaving her his estate, he'd never heard either sister mention any degree of wealth before. They tended toward the eccentric in their dress, but drove a ten-year-old Buick, and had no more, or more expensive looking, jewelry than any of the other ladies in PVC. Neither of them went outside the community very often, other than the occasional trip to Washington to attend concerts at Kennedy Center, and Ed doubted that they rated any kind of news coverage—but, he made a mental note to check that. It made no sense, yet he held the note in his hand. It looked like the real deal.

Ed and Ernesto sat at the dining table while Rose and Peony brought food in from the kitchen. The men offered to help, but were told to sit and pour themselves iced tea. The two women returned, each carrying a platter, one with a stack of toasted tuna sandwiches, the other with a bowl of Caesar salad.

Peony sat at the foot of the small dining table, nearest the kitchen, with Rose opposite her. Ed sat to Peony's left, with Ernesto opposite him. Peony passed the platter of sandwiches to Ed and the salad to Ernesto. The two containers of food arrived in front of Rose at the same time, causing her to pause in confusion while she looked as if she was undecided about which to take first.

When rose noticed that everyone was watching her, she blushed.

"Oh, I'm sorry," she said. "I was thinking of Violet. I guess my mind wandered."

She took a sandwich, and then put a large helping of salad onto the plate next to it.

Ed let everyone eat a few bites before beginning his quizzing of the two women. He didn't take notes. During his twenty five years working as a systems analyst at the Defense Department he'd learned to retain essential information in his memory rather than having to take written notes. His handwriting was so crabby his notes were often indecipherable anyway. By the time they'd finished the salad and sandwiches and were in the living room with glasses of cabernet sauvignon, Ed had gleaned the following scenario from Rose and Peony:

10:30 pm Friday night – Peony had arrived at National Airport from New York City. It took her time to retrieve her bags and get a taxi to bring her to PVC, located on Norbeck Road, four miles north of Georgia Avenue in Montgomery County.

1:15 am Saturday – Peony arrived at the Wertheim home.

7:15 am – Violet and Rose have lunch with Ed and Ernesto at the community center.

8:15 am – Violet and Rose return home.

11:40 am – Rose and Peony go shopping.

12:15 – 12:20 – Rose and Peony return home to find kidnap note.

Ed ran the list of actions through his mind, looking for inconsistencies or relationships. Nothing immediately stood out. No red flags gave him pause. But, his lizard brain itched like crazy, because *something*, what it was he had no idea, just wasn't right. He just couldn't put his finger on it.

Until they heard from the kidnapper, though, there didn't seem to be much he could do. He sat and fidgeted. Then, it occurred to him that he was sitting in the middle of a crime scene, a crime scene that no one had examined.

"Okay, listen up everyone," Ed said. "I want you all to sit right where you are. I'm gonna take a look around and see if there are any clues the kidnapper might have left when he took Violet."

The two women gave him puzzled looks, but Ernesto only nodded.

He started with the living room, checking from the entrance doorway and then around from left to right, looking for anything out of place. There were no indications of any kind of struggle. The windows were all closed and locked, none of the furniture looked to have been moved from where he remembered seeing it the last time he was there, and the four little wooden hampers containing several years' worth of gardening magazines still sat in the corner of the room near the sofa.

"Were the doors locked when you came back from the store?" he asked over his shoulder.

"Yes, both front and back doors were locked. The front still had the security chain in place," Rose responded.

He rubbed his chin, looked around once more and moved on to the dining room. Nothing out of place there—same for the kitchen. He checked the door carefully to see if there'd been any attempts to get at the lock—nothing. The kitchen itself was as neat as a pin. A spatula and spoon in the sink were the only things out of place. The trash bin was empty and looked like it had been washed, something that the sisters did much to the amusement of their neighbors, but Rose always insisted that cleanliness was next to godliness.

He went back to the living room.

"Rose, you mind if I check the bedrooms?"

"Uh, I don't know, Ed," she said. "I mean, a man going into a lady's boudoir-"

"Oh, Aunt Rose," Peony said. "Don't be such a prude. He's just investigating."

"We-l-l-l, I suppose so, but you stay out of my unmentionables, Edward Lazenby."

He checked both bedrooms and their adjoining bathrooms, avoiding the drawers, and saw the same as he'd seen in the rest of the house—a whole lot of nothing.

Back in the living room, he sat on the chair at the right of the sofa and put his hands on his knees.

"Not much we can do now," he said. "But, sit and wait."

FIVE

After an hour of strained silence, Peony made a snorting noise and stood.

"Anyone feel like a cup of coffee?"

"Yeah, I could use one," Ed said. "Need help?"

"No, I can handle it."

She disappeared into the kitchen. A few seconds later, they heard a clatter and a muffled squeak. Ed beat Ernesto through the door into the kitchen by seconds to find Peony standing staring at the base of the kitchen door, her right hand over her mouth.

"What's wrong?" Ed asked.

She pointed downward. A sheet of paper had been slipped partway under the door. Ed reached down and picked it up.

TELL THE PVC MANAGEMENT

Butterfly Effect

TO HIRE A NEW COOK
OR VIOLET WERTHEIM
WILL DIE! WE WILL BE IN TOUCH

Like the first note, this one consisted of words and letters cut from a slick magazine and glued to a piece of plain bond. Ed handled it carefully so that if they ever did get the police involved it could be dusted for fingerprints. Not that he expected there to be any.

"Did you see who did this?" he asked Peony.

"No, it was there when I came in, but I didn't notice it at first. What do we do now?"

Everyone looked at Ed. Yet again, the responsibility was being pushed on to him.

"I guess we need to go to the main office and talk to Dr. Vickers," he said.

Roland Vickers, a general practitioner who had specialized in geriatric medicine late in his career, was CEO and major shareholder in Potomac Valley Community, and had been since its founding ten years earlier. A tall, slender, ascetic looking man with an egg-shaped head, close-set eyes, thin lips, and a razor sharp nose, he wore a sour expression on his pale face that looked like he'd just smelled a particularly odor. A workaholic, he could almost always be found in or near his office in the back corner of the one-story building attached to the community center, which was also the location of the community clinic, where he served as the main doctor.

His secretary was not at her desk. A sour

45

faced woman with a disposition even less sunny than her boss, Karen McGillicuddy refused to work on Saturday or Sunday. But, the door to Vickers' office was open and, as Ed had expected, he was there.

Vickers, wearing a gray suit coat, his starched white shirt buttoned up and held around his neck by a red tie, sat behind his large wooden desk reading from a file spread open before him. Several other files were neatly stacked at his left elbow.

He looked up as Ed cleared his throat to get his attention.

"Ah, Mr. Lazenby," Vickers said. "To what do I owe the pleasure of a visit from you? And, I see you've brought someone with you. Mr. Cardoza, Ms. Wertheim . . . ah, I don't believe I've ever met the young lady." He stood and came from behind his desk.

"This is my niece, Peony Lake, Dr. Vickers," Rose said. "She's visiting from New York."

He smiled somewhat wolfishly as he looked from Peony to Rose. "Yes, I can see the family resemblance." He extended a bony hand. "Welcome to Potomac Valley Community, Ms. Lake," he said.

Peony shook his hand. Ed fought back the urge to snort or laugh. Vickers, who had to be in his early sixties, was simpering at Peony; smiling foolishly like a clumsy, acne-infected high school nerd who has finally gotten a chance to speak to the head of the cheerleading squad. He hung onto Peony's hand longer than was necessary, and much longer than she seemed comfortable with. She carefully withdrew from his grasp, smiling weakly at him.

"Uh, thank you," she said, and moved to put Ed between herself and Vickers.

Vickers didn't seem to notice. He took in the others, smiling at Rose and Ed, his smile disappearing—not quite becoming a frown, but not far from it—when his gaze fell upon Ernesto. Ed knew his reaction was to the way Ernesto dressed.

Vickers moved back to his position behind his desk.

"So, what brings you folks here on such a nice October Saturday afternoon?" he asked, looking directly at Ed as he did.

Damn, Ed thought, *why is everyone always looking at me as if I'm responsible for everything that happens?* "Doc, we have a bit of a problem, and we're gonna need your help to solve it."

"Well, of course," Vickers said. "That's what I'm here for. Please have a seat and tell me what you need."

He sat. They sat. Ed began to outline the problem. Vickers' smile faded as soon as Ed mentioned that Violet was missing, and when Ed got to the part about the two notes, his face faded as well, turning the color of bleached parchment. For a moment, after Ed stopped talking, he sat there in his chair, his shoulders squared, his face pale, and his mouth opening and closing. Then, he cleared his throat.

"There really must be some mistake," he

said. "Who would want to kidnap one of our residents?"

"If we knew that we wouldn't need your help," Ed said. "The demand seems a bit strange, too—who'd resort to kidnapping to get you to hire a new cook—not, mind you, that the community wouldn't benefit from it."

"You're right, that is strange. It almost sounds like some kind of prank."

"I'd say so myself, except that Violet *is* missing," Ed said.

"You gonna call the cops?" Ernesto asked.

Spots of color returned to Vickers' cheeks. "No, no police!" He blinked and took a deep breath. "I mean, the kidnapper was clear on that. If we call the police Violet will be killed. Would you want that on your conscience?"

"But, you just said you thought it was a prank," Ernesto said.

Ed knew his friend was just baiting Vickers, but he found the man's reaction a bit strange. He *had* just said he thought it was a prank, but at the mention of calling the police, a look of worry had flashed across his face.

"It might be," Vickers said. "But, can we afford to take that chance with a woman's life?"

He couldn't disagree with that logic, but something still bothered Ed. Something was off about this whole case.

"Wait a minute," Ed said. "It just occurred to me—the kidnapper's demand—why would a kidnapper demand you hire a new cook? Only one reason. That note is from a resident."

"Why Mr. Lazenby . . . Ed," Vickers said. "Surely you're not accusing one of our residents of such a heinous thing?"

Out of the corner of his eye Ed noticed that Rose's cheeks had gone red, and Peony was looking at him with a strange expression on her face.

"Actually," he said. "It makes perfect sense when you stop and think about it." Now, even Ernesto looked confused. "Who else but someone living here would demand that you hire a new cook?"

"Ah, I see what you mean," Vickers said. He smiled. "That might mean that Ms. Wertheim's actually in no real danger. All the more reason not to involve the police, don't you think?"

Ed glared at Vickers. The man was more focused on not involving the police than on determining Violet Wertheim's fate. But, Ed had to reluctantly concede that, arrogantly uncaring or not, he had a point. If this was indeed some idiotic ploy by community residents trying to improve the quality of the food served in the community center dining room, Violet was unlikely to be in any real danger, and involving the police would only bring unnecessary grief and get a bunch of well-meaning, but misguided fools in trouble.

"I agree with Dr. Vickers . . . for now," he said. "We need to know more about what's going on before we get the police involved."

Vickers looked relieved.

"But," Ed continued. "I think you should

consider doing what the kidnapper asks, and announce that you're going to hire a new cook."

"B-but, we don't have the budget for . . . uh, that would be an insult to Janet Murphy . . . I don't like-"

Ed raised a finger and pointed it at Vickers' face.

"Look, I said announce it. Although, it wouldn't hurt to have someone in the kitchen here who can actually cook," he said. "Not that I'm insulting Ms. Murphy, understand. She's a nice girl, but her cooking is . . . well, let's just say she'd be better sticking to being a dietitian."

"I . . . don't . . . know. Extra staff is expensive."

Peony exploded from the couch. She rushed to Vickers' desk and placed both hands on the surface, leaning forward and fairly spitting her words at him. "You cheap ass son of a bitch! My aunt's in danger and you're worried about the expense? Why, I should hire a lawyer and sue your sorry ass off."

Vickers reacted as if she'd struck him. He raised his hands in surrender, his face twisted in shock as he looked from her to Ed. Ed placed a hand on her shoulder.

"Take it easy, Peony," he said. "I'm sure Dr. Vickers didn't mean to sound so callous."

"N-no, of course not," Vickers said. "I just meant that . . . I have to consider the welfare of everyone here in the community. We have to watch expenses, so of course that came to mind. I assure you, I'm concerned about your aunt. Why, she's one of the pillars of our community."

"If you're so concerned, why don't you just hire a cook?"

Everyone, except Peony who was still glaring down at Vickers, turned in surprise. Rose Wertheim sat straight in her chair, her gaze at Vickers level, her voice steady.

"You say you're so concerned about Violet, but if you really meant it, you'd just hire a new cook and be done with it. In fact, if you really cared about any of us, you'd have hired a real cook long ago. I like Janet. She's a nice girl, but she can't boil water without ruining the taste. If you ate in the dining room you'd know that."

Rose's outburst surprised Ed. It surprised everyone—except perhaps Peony. She'd always been the quiet one of the two sisters, always walking in Violet's shadow, and never expressing her own opinion about anything. She'd certainly never spoken up like this before. Ernesto smiled broadly at her.

"You tell him, Rosie," he said.

"She does have a point, Doc," Ed said.

Vickers seemed to shrink in his chair. It was hard to tell which was affecting him more, Peony's aggressive stance at his desk, or the verbal assaults he was getting from three sources. His brow wrinkled. His lips quivered. He looked like he wanted to cry.

"I'll have to . . . consult the . . . board," he said. "This isn't a decision I can make . . . unilaterally."

Peony folded her arms across her small breasts.

"Don't take too long," she said. "If something happens to my aunt because of you dicking around, I'm going to be very unhappy."

The way Vickers' face paled as she spoke, it became clear that it was Peony who scared him most.

SIX

They left Vickers to do whatever it was he'd
have to do. Peony warned him that if he
didn't make a decision in an hour, she'd be
back. When she said it, she sounded to Ed
like a female version of the cyborg character
played by the actor turned governor, but no
less spooky for being female.

By unspoken agreement they wound up
back at the Wertheim residence. Ed, Ernesto
and Peony sat in the living room. Rose
excused herself and went to the kitchen to
prepare snacks, claiming that it would help
her cope with the stress of not knowing what
Violet's condition was. Ed thought she was
remarkably calm under the circumstances.

"Have you ever known Rose to be so in
control?" he asked Ernesto as soon as Rose
was out of earshot.

Wrinkling his brow in concentration,
Ernesto glanced toward the kitchen.

"Yeah, now you mention it, she really
showed some guts back there in Vickers'

office. Didn't know my Rosie had it in her."

"*Your* Rosie?" Peony whirled around, her faces inches from Ernesto's. "Just what is that supposed to mean?"

"Uh, nothing, it's just . . . you know . . . something I say." He looked to Ed for help.

"Yeah, Peony, that's just the way Ernesto talks."

She looked from Ernesto to Ed and back to Ernesto.

"So, my aunt's not good enough for you?"

Ed sighed and shrugged. Peony was definitely related to Violet and Rose. She was all over the place. Ernesto shrank back against the arm of the sofa and for once, wisely, kept his mouth shut.

Peony looked as if she wanted to say more. Her mouth opened and then snapped shut. She faced forward, folder her arms across her chest and stuck her chin in the air.

It looked to Ed that the two of them had reached a stage of détente, and that he wouldn't have to pull them apart. This was time for him to consider the things that were bothering him. Something about this so-called kidnapping was nagging away at him. He needed answers, and he wasn't even sure what the questions were.

He got up and made his way to the kitchen. Rose was standing in the middle of the room, facing the sink. She held a wrinkled piece of paper in her hand. Her hand was shaking, and there were beads of sweat on her forehead. When she looked up and saw Ed standing there, she opened her eyes wide and held the paper up.

"What is it, Rose?"

"It's another ransom note," she said. She handed it to Ed.

The paper was plain white paper, but seemed different from the first two notes, and instead of the text being cut out of magazines, it was roughly scribbled in pencil.

> We got Violet. We want
> $500,000 or we will kill
> her. Don't call the cops!
> We'll be in touch with you
> so stay close to a phone.

"Where did you find this?" Ed asked.

"It was just like the last one. Someone had slipped it under the door."

Ed held it up in front of her face.

"But, Rose, this is *not* just like the last one, or the one before, and you know it."

"W-what do y-you mean?"

She tried looking innocent and confused, but Ed wasn't buying. She refused to meet his gaze as she played with the blue hair. What she was now was scared. He could smell the fear. And that, he now knew, was what had been missing. Up till now, Rose hadn't displayed any signs of fear.

"Come on, Rose, you know what I'm talking about." Then, the thought slammed into his brain like a test car hitting the crash wall in one of those TV commercials. Violet had been agitating for a cook to prepare palatable meals for some time now, and this was just the kind of stunt she would pull. Rose, of course, ever in her older sister's shadow, would go along. "Rose, tell me the truth," he said. "Violet hasn't really been kidnapped, has she? She's just hiding somewhere, right?"

The deep red blush of her cheeks and the way her eyes refused to come up to look at him told Ed he'd hit the target. He grabbed her by the shoulders and shook her.

"Where is she, Rose?"

"She's out back in the garage."

Ed started at the sound of Peony's voice behind him. He turned to see her standing in the doorway, a wolfish smile on her face. Ernesto stood behind her looking confused.

"Damn," she said. "Aunt Violet said you were good at solving puzzles, but you got this one even quicker than I would have thought possible. What gave us away?"

"Oh, I don't know. It was a lot of little things that didn't quite add up," Ed said. "The biggest of the small things, though, was that ridiculous demand for a new cook at the community center. What the hell kind of kidnapper asks for something like that?"

"I told you and Violet that would never work, and that you should have asked for money," Peony said.

"B-but, we don't need money," Rose said weakly.

Ernesto squeezed past Peony.

"Excuse me, dear," he said. He stood in front of Ed, his hands on his ample hips. "Now, amigo, could you tell me what the hell you people are talking about?"

"Violet wasn't kidnapped, pardner," Ed said.

"I kinda got that . . . I guess, but what the hell's going on?"

Ed turned to Peony who was now standing next to Rose. "Ladies?" he said.

"Okay, you got us," she said. "Aunt Violet thought it would be a way to force these dickheads to finally get someone in the community center who could do more than boil water."

"Actually, poor Janet Murphy doesn't even do that too well," Ed said. "But, staging a kidnapping was a pretty stupid thing to do."

Peony's face turned red. She balled up her fists and stuck her jaw out.

"I am not stupid. Nor is Aunt Violet stupid. This was her idea, and I fully support it."

"Hmph, you're just lucky Vickers is such a stick in the mud bureaucrat," Ed said. "If he'd called the cops, do you realize the trouble you three would be in? Filing a false report of a crime *is* a crime, my dears."

Rose's eyes started blinking rapidly. Peony's mouth dropped open.

"Oh, I didn't know that," Peony said meekly.

Rose looked from her niece to Ed. "They wouldn't really put us in jail for this, would they?"

Ed felt a flash of anger. He was tempted to say yes, but he knew the realities of the justice system. Two old ladies like Violet and Rose would probably just get a slap on the wrists, if a local DA even decided to prosecute—which he doubted.

"Probably not," he said. "But, your neighbors wouldn't be too happy if your little trick had the cops crawling all over the place."

Rose's mouth made a little circle, and her eyes almost crossed.

"I g-guess we never thought about that."

"Damn!" Ernesto said. "Who would have ever thought they had it in 'em?"

Ed looked at Rose. She still looked shaky, and he didn't think it was because of what he'd said about the police.

"There's something else, though, isn't there, Rose?"

"Uh, maybe . . . I'm not sure." She looked at the note Ed was still holding.

He held the note up.

"What is it about this note, Rose?"

"T-that's not Violet's writing," she said.

SEVEN

"Rose, you'd better tell me where Violet is," Ed said.

On the way to where Violet was hiding, their garage of all places, the two women began filling Ed in on their bizarre plot.

Violet had decided that enough was enough, Rose began, and wanted to force Roland Vickers to make changes in the kitchen at the community center. She had approached him with the idea, but had been rebuffed. It was in a phone call with Peony that the idea of faking a kidnapping had been hatched. Peony didn't remember clearly which of them had come up with it first, but recalled thinking it was a great idea and would teach that 'Vickers prick' a good lesson. After their brunch with Ed and Ernesto, Rose and Violet had returned home. Violet had taken a stack of magazines, a ream of paper, some scissors and glue, and gone into the garage where she began manufacturing her kidnap notes. The notes were slipped under the garage door where either Rose or Peony could retrieve them and 'find' them under the kitchen door.

Ed just shook his head as they talked. As much as Vickers deserved being taken down a peg or three, their idea was sheer lunacy, with no chance of success.

Just how stupid it was became clear when Rose lifted the garage door.

Peony made a squeaking sound, like a tiny rodent.

Rose said, "Oh my."

"What the-," interjected Ernesto.

Ed's left eyebrow formed a slight arch upwards. He scrunched his eyes and scanned the scene before him, cataloguing and beginning a mental assessment of the significance of what he was viewing.

The ladies' blue Buick was parked in its customary space, slightly to the right side of the garage, leaving room for storage of tools and other items on the left. They used a lawn service, so there was no lawn mower, nor did they have the other tools one needed to care for a yard, beyond a hoe, rake, and a few trowels they used in tending to their flowers, leaving the left side of the garage normally bare.

It was now cluttered.

Copies of *Better Homes and Gardens*, *Good Housekeeping*, and *Martha Stewart's*

Living were scattered about, some lying open showing that large blocks had been cut from their pages. Among the clutter of magazines was a pair of black-handle sewing scissors, a ream of bond paper that had been torn open, but looked to be still almost full, and an overturned jar of *Elmer's* glue. A folding plastic chair, from the set Ed had seen before on the sisters' patio, was leaned against the garage wall. An overturned plastic pitcher was near the chair, a dark stain of moisture from the edge of the pitcher spout to the baseboard marking its spilled contents. Next to the pitcher was a clear plastic cup, strangely undisturbed, with about half an inch of brown liquid still in it.

It looked as if someone had hastily departed, knocking things asunder in the process, or, heaven forbid, Ed thought, someone had been removed involuntarily from the scene, that someone being Violet Wertheim.

"She's not here," Rose said. "She's supposed to be right here."

Ed continued mentally recording the scene. No blood signs. Good. No Violet. Not good.

"Who besides the two of you knew she was here?" he asked.

"No one," Peony volunteered.

"Did anyone else know about this cockamamie plan?"

"Not unless her phone was tapped. You

don't think her phone was tapped, do you?" Ed shook his head. "We discussed it on the phone on Thursday, and made the final arrangements after I arrived, so I don't know how anyone else could know about it. You two are closer to my aunts than anyone, and you didn't know."

"Yes," Rose said. "We kept it pretty close. We made the final decision just after you and Ernesto went off to play golf this morning. I don't see how anyone else could possibly know."

Ed snapped his finger. "We just left Dr. Vickers' office. He knows about the so-called kidnapping. I wonder . . ."

"You think he came here and snatched Aunt Violet?"

"No, I don't think *he* did. Of course, we can't rule out him getting someone else to do it."

The problem with that theory, Ed knew, was the timing. Vickers wouldn't have had much time to get in touch with someone, locate Violet, and kidnap her. And, of course, there was the new note. It wasn't the type wording a stuff shirt like Vickers would use, and the writing was too neat. Like most doctors, Vickers wrote in an almost illegible scrawl.

"So, what do we do now?" Peony asked.

"Let's start with where we think Violet is," Ed said. "Would she have left the garage for any reason?"

"She wasn't supposed to. She was to stay here and do the notes on schedule, and slip them under the kitchen door where we could find them."

Ed held the handwritten note up again.

"Is this one of her notes?"

Rose shook her head.

"No way! Violet would never scribble a note like that. And, look at the way the paper is crinkled."

"If she didn't do it," Ed said. "That means someone else knows what you're doing and is taking advantage of it."

Peony's face turned ashen. "But, that means-"

"That," Ed said. "Means that Violet has actually been kidnapped."

EIGHT

Ed's words struck like a bolt of lightning. Mouths dropped open. Faces paled. Even Ernesto, usually ready with a quip at a moment's notice, was silent. The silence in the tiny garage was palpable. The only movement in the small space, dust motes that shimmered and flitted like small fireflies in the light coming through the raised door.

Ernesto finally broke the silence. "So, amigo, what do we do now?

"We have to save Violet," Rose said. There was a hint of panic in her voice. "We have to call the police."

"Hold on a minute, Rose," Ed said. "We don't know enough yet to involve the police. Don't forget, the note says for us *not* to call them."

"B-but, we can't just sit around and do

nothing." She was almost crying. Her eyes glistened, and her lips quivered.

Ed felt sorry for her. Sure, they'd gotten themselves into this pickle with their crazy scheme, but they were his friends, and he couldn't just do stand idly by and do nothing. His dilemma, though, was deciding what to do. His first order of business was to keep them calm. He needed time to think. If only the kidnapper or kidnappers—for he had to assume there might be more than one person involved—would give him that time.

"I don't plan to do nothing, Rose," he said gently. "But, I need you guys to remain calm. You wait here in case the kidnappers call. There's something I have to do. I'll be back shortly."

He made an effort to keep any sign of worry out of his voice, and it seemed to work. Rose took deep breaths, and appeared to calm down—a little. Peony looked at him suspiciously, which was no surprise. She didn't really know him. Ernesto smiled. Thank goodness for his old friend, Ed thought.

"Ed's right," Ernesto said. "We won't be doing Violet any good if we go off half-cocked. Why don't we go back inside the house and have some nice calming tea and let Ed do his thing."

Ed sighed as Ernesto led the two women away. Peony glanced back over her shoulder just before they entered the kitchen. She had a pleading look in her eyes.

When the kitchen door closed on his three friends, Ed turned his attention back to the garage. He carefully examined the area around the tilted chair. The mess indicated that whoever had been there, Violet he assumed, had been sitting with their back to the wall. He picked the plastic glass up by placing his first two fingers inside and pressing them against the interior to avoid smudging any fingerprints that might be on it, and sniffed. It was tea, the kind the sisters usually drank, and he could smell the sweetness. Violet dumped at least three teaspoons of sugar in each glass she drank. So, he assumed that it had been Violet sitting in the chair. The mutilated magazines, bond paper, scissors and glue indicated that she'd been busy creating the fake kidnap notes. The way things were scattered looked as if someone had come upon her by surprise and grabbed her, tipping the pitcher and chair, and scattering the other materials in the process. Violet wouldn't be one to go quietly. There would have been noise. But, when they were in the house, they'd heard nothing, and just before leaving to talk to Vickers, they'd received one of her notes. So, he thought, that meant she'd been taken while they were away.

That would tend to eliminate Vickers as a suspect, unless he'd called someone immediately after their departure from his office and the kidnapping had taken place during their ten minute walk from his office back to the house. It was a stretch, but Ed knew he couldn't afford to completely ignore it.

Fortunately, there was nothing to indicate Violet had been injured—no blood or torn clothing. That didn't mean she might not have been bruised, but he refused to allow himself to consider that.

His first step would have to be confronting Vickers again.

NINE

Vickers was in the corridor outside his office, talking to Candice Drummond, the community nurse, when Ed arrived.

Drummond was a tall woman, only a half inch shorter than Ed's six feet, with broad shoulders, large breasts, a thin waist, and boyish hips that still looked fetching in the pants of the lime green pantsuit she wore that also set off a pair of athletic legs. Her dark brown hair was worn in a tight bun, accenting her small ears and oval face. She had large, amber colored eyes set wide in her face, giving her a gamin-like appearance. Ed thought she'd be called beautiful but for a slight overbite and a bump midway up her nose that looked like a break that hadn't been properly set, that and the fact that he'd hardly ever seen her smile.

"Dr. Vickers, Nurse Drummond," he said. "How are you this evening? Glad I caught you still in, doc. I need to talk to you about something."

"Can it wait until Monday, Ed," Vickers said. "Candice and I have had a long day, and I was looking forward to a bit of down time. I'm taking Candice to dinner and a concert in DC."

"Afraid it can't doc. It's about . . . that matter we spoke of earlier today."

Vickers and Drummond shared a look. Ed watched them closely, but noticed no signs of nervousness. It was common knowledge around the community that the two were seeing each other, and though they were discreet, they knew that people knew. Vickers cleared his throat.

"Oh, yes . . . that issue," he said. "Candice, would you excuse us? This'll only take a few minutes."

"Sure," she said. "I'll wait for you in the lobby."

Vickers unlocked his office door and motioned Ed inside. As he entered, Ed noticed that Drummond was still standing in the corridor.

Inside the office, Vickers pointed to his visitor's chair.

"Won't you have a seat?"

"Thanks, doc, but this won't take that long. I need to know if you told anyone else about our little . . . situation."

Vickers looked surprised. "Why, no, why would I do that? We agreed not to call the police. Why do you ask?"

Ed detected no indication of lying.

Working in the Pentagon bureaucracy he'd developed a good sense of when people weren't being completely honest with him.

"No special reason," he said. "Just wanted to make sure we were still keeping a lid on this thing until we can sort it out."

"Well, I for one hope you do it soon. I mean, a kidnapping here at Potomac Valley Community would be a bloody disaster for us. The investors wouldn't like that at all. Even a fake kidnapping could have serious financial repercussions."

So like the man to worry more about what the investors might think than for a woman's safety.

"Yeah," Ed said. "And, let's not forget the fact that this might not be a fake kidnapping. Someone might have actually kidnapped Violet."

"Surely, a man with your background doesn't believe this is real, do you? This has all the earmarks of a practical joke by the Wertheim sisters, especially that Violet. She's been something of a thorn in my side from her first day here; always demanding improvements or that we hire extra staff, as if money was no object. Very impractical, I can tell you. She has no idea what it takes to run a business like this."

"Doctor, under the circumstances I don't think we can risk treating this as anything other than real until we know for sure. We're dealing with a woman's life here."

Vickers flinched. Ed knew his tone was harsh, deliberately so. While he was now convinced that Vickers wasn't involved in actually kidnapping anyone, he still didn't trust the man to do the right thing. He'd worked far too long with people like Vickers, people who put bureaucratic procedures before human relations, the bottom line before human life. He wanted to leave no doubt in his mind the seriousness of the situation. His paleness said the message had gotten through. His words confirmed it. "Of course, the welfare of our residents always comes first. My concern, though, is that if we don't call the police, how will we determine what is really going on?"

"I have a small amount of experience doing investigations," Ed said. He didn't say that those were investigations of why certain procedures failed, not criminal activity, but Vickers didn't need to know that. Besides, Ed thought, an investigation is an investigation. The goal is to determine the truth. *Can't be all that different. Yeah, right Ed, keep telling yourself that and you might even start believing it.*

Vickers looked relieved. Whether from a belief that Ed could really successfully resolve the situation, or just that it was no longer his problem, Ed couldn't tell. Actually, it made no difference as long as it kept Vickers in check.

"Very well then, Ed, I'll leave it in your

capable hands. Please let me know when this mess is taken care of."

Well, at least I know it's because he's just glad to pass the buck. "Not to worry, doc, I'll let you know whatever I find out. Hopefully we'll soon be able to put this all behind us. Enjoy your evening out."

As he left Vickers' office Ed noticed that Candice Drummond was still in the corridor. She had her back to Vickers' door, but Ed could have sworn she'd just stepped away from it.

She gave him a curious look as he stepped past her.

TEN

Ed found Ernesto and the two women sitting on the sofa in the Wertheim living room looking as if they hadn't moved from their spots since assuming them. There was a fourth cup, empty, on the coffee table, but when Ed felt the teapot, it was already cold.

"Would anyone like for me to heat the tea up?" he asked.

Rose blinked as if coming out of a trance.

"Oh, my goodness, the tea got cold." She grabbed the teapot and stood. "Sit down, Ed. I'll warm it up."

She scurried out of the room.

"What did you learn from that turd, Vickers?" Peony asked.

Vickers wasn't on Ed's Christmas list, but it upset him just a bit hearing a young person like Peony refer to him in such a manner. But, he decided not to react to it.

"Not much. I'm pretty sure he's not involved with whoever took your aunt . . . oh, and he assured me he hasn't called the police, and he seems happy to leave it to us to get this whole thing sorted out."

"Of course he is," she said. "He's a damned bureaucrat. They're always happy to let someone else take the responsibility, as long as they get the credit. So, what do you plan to do?"

On the walk back from Vickers' office, Ed had given a lot of thought to the situation.

"I've been trying to figure out who might have taken your aunt, and I've pretty much come to the conclusion that it has to be someone from right here in PVC, either staff or resident."

"Why would you think that?"

"In the first place, entry to the community is controlled by two gates—unless you come through the woods to the east and hop the fence, but kidnappers aren't likely to do that. Vans and trucks going in and out are checked. We had some thefts a while back, and the guards are pretty strict about the checks. Believe me, if someone tried getting a body out of here, we'd have known about it by now."

"So, amigo, that means Violet is also somewhere on the grounds," Ernesto said. "Trouble is, those grounds cover over two hundred acres."

"Yeah, yeah, I know, but I doubt they're keeping her outside, so we need to focus on buildings."

"Okay, that leaves over five hundred

places she could be."

Ed scrunched his forehead and stared at his friend through narrowed slits of his lids.

"You're just a lot of help, aren't you? Look I know there are a lot of buildings here, but we can eliminate many of them. For instance, the community center, too many people coming and going, most of the residences right around here, for the same reason."

Ernesto's eyes scrunched up. "Ah, I see where you're coming from. That still leaves a lot of buildings, but a lot less than five hundred."

"Furthermore," Ed said. "We can start to rule out anyone who hasn't been in close contact with Rose and Violet for the past two or three days."

"That pretty much rules out just about everyone who lives here but you and me, compadre."

Ed thought about that for a moment. Then, he snapped his fingers.

"You're right, old buddy," he said. "It couldn't be a resident, because Rose and Violet never socialize with any of the other residents."

"That's not completely true," Rose said, coming back into the living room carrying a teapot. "Tea anyone? Violet and I participate in the flower show every spring. We talk to lots of people then."

Ed and Ernesto looked at each other and smiled. Rose set about refilling everyone's cup.

"So," Ernesto said. "It has to be someone on the staff, right?"

"That's the way I see it."

"Well, that's a more manageable problem. All we gotta do is figure out which staff the gals came into contact with the past few days, what buildings they have access to, and we swoop in and rescue Violet."

Ed took a sip of tea. It was jasmine, one of his favorites.

"Something like that, I suppose," he said. "Now, let's start making that list."

Peony had been sitting quietly sipping her tea until that point.

"You guys need some paper and something to write with?" she asked.

Ed smiled. "That would be nice."

She bounced up and headed toward the bedrooms. A few minutes later she came back with a blue spiral notebook and a handful of yellow number 2 pencils, which she placed on the coffee table. When Ernesto picked up a pencil and frowned, she laughed.

"What's the matter, big man, haven't you ever used a pencil before?"

He snorted.

"Of course I have. I was just expecting a ballpoint or something."

"Actually, that's a good idea," Ed said. "That way, it's easier to make corrections."

Peony stuck her tongue out at Ernesto. He laughed.

Before they could begin listing names, the doorbell rang. Rose went to the door, and looked through the window at the side.

"There's a scruffy looking man out here," she said. "Uh-oh, he's holding up a badge."

"Montgomery County Police," a man's muffled voice said from outside. "I'm looking for Edward Lazenby or Rose Wertheim."

"Oh, shit," Ernesto said.

"Guess you'll have to let him in, Rose," Ed said, shrugging.

She opened the door.

"Yes, may I help you?" she asked.

"I'm Detective Sergeant Carl Janzen, Montgomery County Police," the man standing there said as he held up his badge. He was wearing a rumpled brown suit, wore black shoes that were scuffed and in need of polish, needed a shave, and had black hair, streaked with white, that looked as if he'd just gotten out of bed. His brown eyes were bloodshot, with dark circles under them. "Are you Rose Wertheim?"

"Yes, I am, detective. What can I do for you?"

Janzen walked in, nodding his head at Rose as he passed her. He looked at Ed and Ernesto, not so much frowning as curious.

"One of you guys Edward Lazenby?" he asked, ignoring Rose.

Ed stood. "Yeah, I'm Ed Lazenby."

Janzen's gaze swept the room. He adjusted the collar of his rumpled jacket.

"MCPD got a call stating there'd been a possible kidnapping here," he said. "What can you tell me about it?"

Just like that. No preliminaries, no introductions, no warning. A good way to throw people off their guard. Ed's first impression of the man and his crumpled suit had been negative, but Janzen's ploy raised him in Ed's estimation. Rumpled he might be on the outside, but there was a sharp mind behind those bloodshot eyes.

Of course, Ed was no stranger to these kinds of mind games.

"Where did you hear that, sergeant?" he asked.

Janzen gave him a piercing look.

"If you don't mind, Mr. Lazenby, I'll ask the questions," he said. "*Has* there been a kidnapping here?"

Ed decided that it would do no good trying to play games with the man, and he had no desire to get ensnared in accusations of interfering with a criminal investigation.

"Uh, we're not sure, detective," he said. "Our friend, Violet Wertheim, Rose's older sister, is missing. We have a note demanding money and warning us not to go to the police."

"Sounds like a kidnapping to me," Janzen said. "When did you discover her missing?"

He whipped a notebook and pen from his jacket pocket, straddled an empty chair facing the sofa across the coffee table, and began jotting down notes as they talked.

Ed began by telling him what they knew—leaving out any reference to the sisters' fake kidnapping plot, and giving cutting looks at the others to make sure they noticed that omission. He carefully took the 'real' ransom note from his pocket, holding it with his fingers pinching a tiny bit of a corner. Janzen's expression as he watched was interesting. He seemed to be examining Ed in a different, more positive light.

"This is the note we found shoved under the kitchen door," Ed said as he placed the paper on the coffee table.

Janzen leaned forward, reading the note without touching it.

"Who else touched this?" he asked.

"Well, other than me, and whoever wrote it, only Rose," Ed replied.

Janzen fumbled around in his jacket, finally extracting a pair of latex gloves and a large snap-seal plastic bag. He donned the gloves and carefully slid the note inside the bag. He wrote some cryptic notes on a small card he took from his pants pocket, and put that in the bag with the note, sealed the bag, and stuffed it into the inside pocket of his jacket.

"Okay," he said. "Now, start at the beginning and tell me everything."

While Janzen had first appeared unimpressive; in fact, Ed thought he resembled the Peter Falk character in the old

1970s 'Columbo' TV show, it soon became clear that his ruffled exterior concealed a quick, analytical mind. He was methodical in his questioning; stopping them frequently to clarify points, and Ed noticed that his writing was precise and easy to read. It took an effort to avoid disclosing Violet's fake kidnapping scheme. Several times, when it looked as if Rose or Peony might say something damaging, Ed interrupted them to answer Janzen's questions. Each time he did this, though, the detective gave him a funny look.

Finally, after the longest hour of Ed's life, Janzen flipped his notebook close and put it back in his pocket.

"I'd like to take a look at the garage now," he said. He looked from Ed to Rose. "Ms. Wertheim, you look a bit frazzled. Maybe Mr. Lazenby can show me. You do know the layout, don't you, Mr. Lazenby?"

"Sure, sergeant, I can show you. I've been here a lot, and the layout of all the houses is the same anyway." Ed stood. "Peony, why don't you make another pot of tea for Rose and Ernesto. I'm sure this'll only take a few minutes."

"Y-yeah," Peony said. "That sounds like a good idea. Would you like a cup of tea, sergeant?"

Janzen paused. His gaze as he looked at Peony was unreadable.

"Yeah, I suppose I could have a cup of tea," he said. "We'll be back in a few minutes.

After you, Mr. Lazenby."

They walked in silence through the kitchen. At the door, Janzen paused and examined the door, paying particular attention to the floor around the base. He then stood aside to allow Ed to lead him to the garage, and once there, waited while Ed lifted the door.

"This is where she was when she . . . it happened," he said. "Is this how you found the place?"

Ed looked around. Everything seemed to be where he'd first seen things.

"Yeah, this is what I remember."

Janzen walked in, careful not to step on any of the scattered magazines. He knelt and looked closely at one that had been particularly mutilated. He then stood and faced Ed.

"Looks like somebody was cutting stuff out of these magazines."

"Yeah, I noticed that too," Ed said. "Violet kept scrap books. Maybe she was cutting things out."

Janzen rubbed a hand over his stubbled cheek.

"Is that so? Don't seem to be any pictures cut out, though. Seems like words or letters, like maybe somebody was cutting out words to make notes." He pointed at the scissors and glue.

"Now that you mention it, that does seem to be the case, doesn't it?"

Lazenby took the plastic bag from his coat and held it up in front of Ed's face.

"But, this ransom note's written in pencil," he said. "I don't see a pencil anywhere here, do you?"

Damn, he's sharp. "Uh, no, I don't."

He put the bag back into his pocket, and put his hands on his hips.

"Okay, Lazenby, you want to tell me what's really going on here?" There was a note of command in his voice.

The crunch had come. Ed knew, knew deep down in his bones that Janzen was no fool; that he somehow knew information was being withheld. He felt a sense of loyalty to his friends, and keeping quiet about Violet's foolish ploy, while technically a lie, was a whole different matter than actually *telling* a lie. Despite the general attitude toward policemen since the militarization following September 11, 2001, and the many cases of police overreaction, he still had a lot of respect for those who were willing to put their lives and safety on the line for common citizens like him, and he would not, under any circumstances—at least, any that he could think of—deliberately lie to a cop.

So, he told Janzen what he knew of what had transpired. From Violet's plan to coerce Vickers to hire a cook who actually knew how to cook by pretending to be kidnapped, to them returning to the house and finding that she was actually gone.

"Look," he said. "I know what the girls did was wrong, illegal in fact, but none of us actually reported to the police, so you can't say they really falsely reported a crime."

Janzen frowned and made a growling sound deep in his throat. "Technically, you're right, but damn it, I still oughta run you people in. Faking a kidnapping just to get better food! That sounds like something cons do in stir, not old people in a retirement community. And now, you've got a real kidnapping on your hands."

Ed felt chastened, but he would *not* let Janzen know that.

"It's not like we, I mean they, planned for this to happen. By the way, who called you and reported this?"

"Sorry, I'm not at liberty to disclose that information."

Ed had an idea who'd done it. Either Vickers was better at lying than he thought, and he'd done it, or . . . Candice Drummond! Yes, Ed thought, she had been listening at the door. He didn't know the nurse that well, not being much in need of her services, or any other medical professional for that matter, but she and Vickers were the only ones he could say for sure knew what Violet and Rose had been up to. She might have heard him through the door when he and Vickers were discussing the 'kidnapping.'

"Okay, I can respect that," he said. "So, what next?"

"Well, the first thing is I'll have to get the lab in to process this scene."

Ed pointed at Janzen's coat. "What about the kidnapper's instructions not to call the police? Won't that endanger Violet?"

"Ah, yeah, there is that." Janzen stood still for a few seconds, looking up at the ceiling of the garage, studying the pulley mechanism that opened the door. "Okay, here's how we'll handle that. I'll have the lab boys come in a lawn service van."

"We have our own people to take care of lawns," Ed said. "Do you have an air conditioning or heating repair van? That would explain them going inside the structure."

Janzen's face contorted like someone who has just bit into a sour lemon, then relaxed.

"Yeah, I guess that makes more sense," he said. He pulled out his mobile phone and hit speed dial. After a few moments he spoke into the phone, almost too fast for Ed to follow, then rang off. "Okay, the lab boys will be here in fifteen or twenty minutes."

"There's one other thing, sergeant. Could you keep the uniformed police away . . . for a while at least, or until we know Violet's safe?"

"Look, Lazenby, I don't need you telling me . . . oh, hell, you've got a point. Okay, for now, it's just me and the lab guys. Now, let's go back inside. I don't want to attract attention standing around here too long."

That made sense. Ed led him back to the

kitchen. Rose came out and fussed over them until both agreed to have a cup of tea. What Ed wanted, though, was for the police to do their CSI thing and make themselves scarce. He worried that there'd be a slip up, and Violet's abductors would be spooked into doing something drastic. Lazenby, though, kept looking at him with a kind of squinty eyed look that made Ed nervous.

"Anything else we can do for you, sergeant?" Ed asked, and instantly regretted speaking. He knew he was coming across as nervous.

"Is there something else you think you *should* be doing, Mr. Lazenby?"

Damn, what a rookie mistake to make. "No, not really, I was just wondering . . . you know-" *Shut your fricking mouth Ed Lazenby!* "No, sergeant, I think we've told you all we know."

"Well, I probably should be putting a trace on Ms. Wertheim's phone, for when the kidnapper calls back."

"Will that involve having a lot of police hanging around?"

"You've been watching too much TV, Mr. Lazenby," Janzen said. "We only need one guy to monitor the trace, and he wouldn't be in uniform."

"I guess that's okay. I'll of course let you know whatever I learn."

Janzen's brow wrinkled. "If you're hinting that you plan to do some snooping on your own, Lazenby, let me tell you right up front—don't do it! This is no time for an amateur stumbling around. You're just likely to get the victim killed, or get yourself killed. So, stay the hell out of our way."

Well, if that's the way you're gonna be. "Of course, sergeant," Ed said. "I wouldn't think of getting in your way."

"I noticed when I came in that the guards check all vehicles in and seem to be searching those that leave," Janzen said.

Ed nodded. "Yes, we had a few thefts last year. The new security procedures have been in effect since then."

"So, it's unlikely Ms. Wertheim's been taken from the area."

"That's my assumption, sergeant."

Janzen scratched his chin, making a scratchy sound. He then ran his hand through his rumpled hair. A few flakes of dandruff drifted down to the shoulders of his jacket, joining those already there.

"Well, I guess I'll have to have some of my people start canvassing the area," he said.

"Uh, sergeant," Ed said. "You sure that's a good idea. Won't having a bunch of policemen prowling around the community alert the kidnappers?"

"Do I look like I just fell off the turnip truck?" Janzen's frown was patently fake. Ed could tell the man was having him on. "I wouldn't have a bunch of goons in uniform, in fact, I wouldn't even have men. I know a couple of lady cops, young women who look more like girl scouts than cops in fact, who'd be perfect. Might even cover them as girl scouts or something, to give them an excuse to go door to door querying people."

While he wasn't totally comfortable with it, Ed saw no way he could argue against it. A couple of women cops would at least be better than a bunch of uniformed officers, who would be all too likely to get excited and go Rambo on someone, or shoot a dog, which would start a riot in PVC that would make the Watts riots look like a college fraternity prank. Those residents in PVC who owned pets were close to their four-legged family members.

"Okay, just remember," he said. "People here can be pretty sensitive and prickly. If your people come on too strong, or give it away that they're looking for a kidnap victim it'll be all over the community faster than you can say Jack Robinson."

"Jack who?" Janzen asked.

"That's an old—oh, never mind. Just urging you to remind your people to be discrete."

ELEVEN

Janzen's phone tech, who introduced himself as Allan Franklin, a youngster dressed in baggy jeans and a Redskins' sweatshirt who didn't look old enough to shave, showed up and set up his equipment, a laptop computer and a strange looking device Ed had never seen before. He was a bit upset that the sisters didn't have a landline, but said his monitor could deal with mobile phones, it would just take a little juggling to answer the phone when it rang and then put it into a receptacle in the top of the strange looking device, which would then allow them to talk to the caller while the computer, connected to a mainframe computer at police headquarters through a wireless connection, would trace the location of the originating call—provided they could keep the caller on the line long enough.

"How long is long enough?" Ed asked.

"Well, if they're calling from a landline or a registered cell phone, we can ping 'em in 30 seconds," Franklin said, rubbing at a pimple on the point of his chin. "If they're using a prepaid or burner phone, it can take longer, because we have to triangulate their location—about a minute or two . . . maybe."

With that bit of reassurance, Ed felt his misgivings about involving the police returning full force. Of course, the deed was done, so they had no choice but to try and make the best of it; meaning, *he* had to try and make the best of it.

Janzen's two female cops, also looking like they'd just graduated high school, were a bit better. They wore tight jeans and long-sleeved sweaters that accented their figures; guaranteed to cause all the men in the community to gawk and the women to glare. But at least no one was likely to think they were cops.

"I guess that's all we can do now," Janzen said after he'd given the two policewomen their instructions. "I'm going back to headquarters. They'll call me if they find anything, and I can be back here in less than twenty minutes."

"Whatever you do, don't bring S.W.A.T., please," Ed said.

Janzen rolled his eyes. "No way I'm bringing those cowboys in unless we're under siege." He squinted at Ed. "But, I had the boys at HQ run a check on you, Lazenby. You were some kind of detective at the Pentagon, right?"

"I was a systems analyst. That's sort of like a detective, but my job was tracking numbers, not people."

"Okay, just so we're straight on this. I don't want you freelancing on this. Stay out of the way and let us do our jobs."

Ed held his right hand up, three fingers straight and the little pinkie tucked under his thumb. "Scout's honor, sergeant," he said. "I will not get in your way."

Janzen grunted and squinted again. Finally, he shrugged and walked away. Ed let out a breath. He hadn't lied. He had no intention of getting in Janzen's way. He intended to be way out in front of him. He was going to find and rescue Violet and nab the kidnapper.

Ernesto had been standing in the door between the living and dining rooms. When the front door closed behind Janzen, he walked in and put a hand on Ed's shoulder.

"You didn't really mean that, did you?"

"What?"

"That you wouldn't get in his way."

Ed laughed. "Oh, I meant that. I don't plan to get in his way. What I do plan to do is find Violet," he responded in a voice just above a whisper so Franklin wouldn't hear, but the young tech was so absorbed in fiddling with his laptop he never even looked up.

"Now, that's my compadre. When do we get started?"

"Let's get Rose and her niece settled, and we can go to my place and plan our next move."

TWELVE

Rose was busy in the kitchen preparing food and drink for her new houseguest. Peony assisted, but kept going to the dining room where she could peer in at Franklin as he played with his high tech gizmos. Ed let them know that he and Ernesto were going to his house, and for Peony to call if they needed anything, leaving Rose's phone free should the kidnapper call.

Back at Ed's house, they sat on the sofa in his living room, a bottle of Jack Daniels, a bucket of ice cubes, and two glasses on the coffee table. Ed put two cubes and two fingers of bourbon in each glass. Handing one to Ernesto, he lifted the other in a toast.

"Here's to a successful outcome," he said.

"Yeah, *salud*," Ernesto said, downing half the liquor. "So, what do we do first?"

"I've been thinking about it," Ed said. "First we need to find out who might have known about Violet's little scheme. I'm thinking it's not a resident. Hell, you and I are in better condition than anyone else in this dump, and I'm not sure we'd be able to subdue Violet."

"For sure. That woman's a pistol. I'd be afraid she'd rip my eyes out."

"Yeah, there's that. But, there's also the fact that Violet can't keep her mouth shut, and she's got a loud voice. She likely talked about it somewhere it could be overheard."

"So, who would . . . could have overheard her, and why would that make 'em want to kidnap her?"

Ed had been thinking about that. He remembered the way Violet talked at brunch, and wondered if she and Rose had discussed her plot after he and Ernesto went off to play golf.

"It could be someone at the Community Center. One of the staff."

"Jesus! You really think somebody on the staff would do something like that?"

"With security at the gates, no one from outside could have done it. It has to be an inside job; either a resident or staffer. I just have a gut feeling . . . it's someone on the staff. Now, try to remember everyone who was near us during brunch."

Between them, they listed everyone from the community center staff who either came near the table or were on the serving line when they Violet or Rose got food. There were the two women who kept an eye on the line, making sure empty platters were kept filled, an elderly black woman and a young white woman with hair even redder than Rose's, the busboy, a Salvadorian, and the dietitian, Janet Murphy. Ed ran the entire list through his mind. The more he thought about it, the clearer it became, but he didn't want to accept it.

"What's the matter, amigo?" Ernesto asked. "You look like you just swallowed something a bit off."

Ed shook himself. He clenched his eyes tight, going over the names again. *It can't be! But, it's the only thing that makes sense.* "Ernesto, I have an idea who might have . . . no, must have, overheard Violet and Rose talk about their plan," he said. "But, even more; remember the other night at supper when they were talking about Violet inheriting her uncle's fortune?"

"Yeah, that's the first I'd heard of that, too."

"Well, there was someone else who probably heard it for the first time, and as sad as it is to say, it's someone who would also have a motive to do something bad to Violet."

"Naw, man, you can't mean-"

"Afraid I do. Janet Murphy was near the table that night, and had to have heard it. She was also hovering around the tables at brunch. And, you know how Violet's always trashing her cooking."

Ernesto shook his head.

"I . . . she's such a nice girl."

"I hope I'm wrong," Ed said. "But, let's go talk to her."

They polished off their drinks. Ed made sure to lock his door, and they hiked across Wisteria, past the building where art lessons were held, and into the community center. As Ed expected, Janet Murphy was there—she always was—bustling about getting the dining room set up for the next meal. When he and Ernesto walked in and headed toward her, Ed could see several emotions flash quickly across her face. First, her eyes widened in panic, then clouded in fear, but by the time they came abreast of her, where she was adjusting the roses in a vase on the buffet dessert counter, she had her trademark smile in place.

"Hi, guys," she said. Ed detected a twinge of strain in her usually bubbly voice. "You're here early. What's up? Can I make you a snack of something?" The words tumbled out with barely a pause between sentences. Her lips smiled, but her eyes flicked from side to side. She refused to meet Ed's gaze.

Ed could almost feel guilt oozing from her pores. It made him sad. She always seemed like such a nice person.

"No, Janet," he said. "We're not here to eat. We need to talk to you. Is there somewhere we can speak privately?"

Now, the look of fear was back. Now, he could smell the fear, a palpable scent emanating from her body. Her eyes got misty, like she wanted to cry, but she kept the smile on her face, though strained. She looked like she wanted to run, but there was nowhere to go.

"W-what do you want to talk about?"

Ed looked around. The only other people in the dining room were the elderly black woman, who was busy stacking plates on a wheeled cart in the far corner, and the busboy; at the entrance sweeping and whistling some unidentifiable tune. Nonetheless, Ed didn't want their conversation overheard.

"It's something we really need to discuss in private, Janet. Trust me."

The skittish look in her eyes told Ed that trusting him was the last thing on her mind, but she finally nodded weakly.

"Okay, we can go back to my office."

They followed her through the dining room into the six-foot-long vestibule that led to the kitchen. The space was about four feet wide, with doors on either side. One door was marked 'Pantry,' and the other 'Janitorial Supplies.' The sound of their shoes on the wooden parquet floor echoed around them, and Ed could hear the tinkle of plates from the front of the dining room as the elderly woman moved them around. It was like being in an echo chamber. He could imagine someone standing in this space, not in clear sight of anyone dining in the main area, able to hear all but the most hushed conversations taking place in the large rectangular dining area. Violet's strident voice, and the fact that she seldom tried keeping it down even when she was slamming someone nearby, would have been easily heard by anyone standing there.

The kitchen was quiet. The redhead was standing at the big restaurant-sized stove off to the left, idly stirring something in a large aluminum pot with a wooden ladle. She wore earphones attached to an MP-3 player attached to a belt around her thin waist, and didn't even look up as they passed. Ed didn't recognize the aroma coming from the steaming pot, but decided that he'd forgo his usual supper in the dining facility and just make a peanut butter and spam sandwich at home. Ernesto wrinkled his nose. Murphy didn't seem to notice the odor. She kept darting her gaze from the floor in front of her back over her shoulder at Ed and Ernesto.

She passed through a swinging door at the back of the kitchen and they entered another vestibule of the same dimensions as the one at the front, but with doors at both ends. On the left was a large, thick metal door with a small glass window centered about five feet from the floor and a large push bar across the middle. The icy rime on the window identified this as the cold storage room. Directly across from it was another door, normal sized and wooden. Murphy opened that door and went in, leaving it open for the two men. Neither door had a sign.

Murphy's office was only slightly larger than a storage closet. A small metal desk with a swivel chair behind it sat in the middle. To the right of the desk was a three-shelf bookcase filled with stacks of magazines and several large binders. Looking closely, Ed saw that they were cookbooks, mostly from *Good Housekeeping, Rachel Ray,* and *Martha Stewart,* with titles like *Desserts Made Easy, How to Cook for Large Crowds*, and the like. An open binder and a yellow legal size notepad lay on the desk. The binder was a recipe book. Murphy hurried behind her desk, grabbed the binder and snapped it shut, and then put it and the pad on the floor beside her chair.

"Sorry I can't offer you guys seats," she said. "I don't get visitors, so I only have the one chair."

"That's okay," Ed said. "I just have a few questions. It won't take long."

"Good. I have to start getting ready for the meal." She glanced quickly down at the binder. "What do you want to ask me?"

"Last night and this morning, when Ernesto and I ate here with Violet and Rose Wertheim, do you recall what we talked about?"

She fidgeted and played with the collar of

her blouse, looking down at her desk. Ed had seen this kind of reaction before, always by someone who was thinking about telling a lie.

"Uh, what you were talking about? Well, I wasn't near all that much . . . last night, and this morning, you say?"

Another sign of evasion, repeating the question. She was stalling for time while she worked out a lie—he knew it.

"Yes, do you remember what we talked about last night?"

She took a deep breath.

"Well, Violet was insulting my cooking . . . like she does most of the time. Last night and this morning as well."

"Oh," Ernesto said. "You know Violet. Her bark's worse than her bite. I'm sure she doesn't mean half the things she says."

"She meant it all right. She always means it." Her eyes glistened. "Trouble is, she's right. I know I'm not the best cook in the world, but I can't get Dr. Vickers to hire a real cook. I do the best I can with Darlene and Martha, but none of us are used to cooking meals for so many people. It's just not the same as cooking for one or two."

She didn't meet Ed's eyes as she spoke. He sensed that there was more, that she was withholding something.

Ed leaned forward, his hands splayed on her desk and his face only two feet from hers. She shrunk back, her face pale.

"Now, Janet," he said. "You heard more

than that."

"What more could I have heard?"

"I don't know. Why don't you tell me?"

Her mouth opened and closed. She clenched her eyes shut. Opened the left eye to look up at Ed. Then, she opened both eyes and sighed.

"Well, I did hear her talking about her Uncle Morrison, no, Mortimer . . . I heard her saying that he'd left her his fortune. That was last night."

"What did you hear this morning?"

"Just more complaining about my cooking."

"What about after Ernesto and I left the dining room?"

"Nothing, they left almost immediately after the two of you."

This time, there was no hesitation. Ed felt she was being truthful about that. So, she probably knew nothing about Violet's kidnap scheme. She couldn't, therefore, have been piggybacking on it.

"Wait a minute," he said. "Did you repeat any of what you heard to anyone else?"

Her eyes went wide and her face paled even more.

"You did, didn't you?"

Her lips quivered. Small tears formed in the corner of her eyes.

"W-well, I . . . I might have mentioned it to my boyfriend."

"Where can we find this boyfriend?" Ed

asked.

"Oh . . . I'm not sure I should-"

"Look, Janet, this is important. I can't explain why right now, but I think it'd be better that you tell me than have to tell the police."

"P-police . . . w-why would the p-police be interested in what I say to my boyfriend?" Now, her face was wet with a combination of sweat and tears. Her whole body was shaking.

"I think you know why, Janet," Ed said. "If you tell me everything now, maybe we can help you."

"B-but, I haven't done anything," she said in a whining voice.

"Where can I find your boyfriend, Janet?"

She wrapped her arms around her chest and leaned forward. "At the g-golf course," she said. "It's Lou, Lou Palmer."

"When did you tell him?"

"Last night. We were at his house around midnight, I guess. We were just sitting around having a drink and talking, and I guess it just slipped out, you know. I told him about how Violet was always going on about my cooking and how it upset me."

"How did he take it?"

"Oh, you know . . . well, maybe you don't," she said. "He was pretty miffed, you know. He said these rich bitches are always looking down their noses at the rest of us, and he'd like to shove their noses in it."

"Do you think he'd do anything to hurt Violet?"

"I d-don't know," she said, looking down at the floor. "I mean, he was upset last night, but I haven't talked to him yet today . . . we didn't spend the night together or anything like that. It might have just been the wine talking . . . you know."

What Ed *knew* was that she was trying to convince herself that what she was saying was true—and, not doing a good job of it.

"Come on, Ernesto," he said. "We need to get over to the golf course and talk to Louis Palmer."

THIRTEEN

They didn't find Palmer at the clubhouse, and the guy at the starter shack said he hadn't seen around yet, but that he might be working on someone's yard as he was also responsible for grounds maintenance for the residential areas.

"So, I got two questions," Ernesto said. "How we gonna find this dude, and what we gonna do when we find him?"

"One thing at a time, pardner. First, we have to find him."

"Yeah, just a couple hundred yards to check out. No sweat."

Ed looked at the club's employee parking lot. The maintenance truck was in its usual slot.

"Shouldn't be all that hard," he said. "It has to be close, since his truck's still here."

"Okay, let's do this thing."

They debated splitting up to go faster, or staying together. Even though staying together would take longer, Ernesto knew that Ed was much better at handling people, so the extra time they'd save by going separately would be eaten up by him having to find Ed if he spotted Palmer.

They wound through the back and front yards of the houses closest to the golf course, earning strange looks from the residents who were still at home. At one house, when a short, fat woman, wearing her frizzy white hair in old fashioned curlers, challenged them, they said they were looking for a lost dog. She made a sniffing noise at them, clutched her robe tighter and went back inside her house, muttering something about 'people and their damned pets.'

It was approaching 6:00 pm when they finally spotted Palmer, coming from the direction of one of the condo buildings pushing a wheelbarrow. He was dressed in his blue maintenance overalls with a John Deere cap pulled down over his eyes. Clumps of his greasy brown hair hung over his ears and collar.

He stopped at the corner when Ed waved at him.

"Hey, Mr. Lazenby," he said as they came up to him. "Mr. Cardoza. What you two doing out this time of evening? Shouldn't you be up at the dining hall? I hear Janet's planning a special treat tonight."

"We need to ask you something," Ed said. "Do you have time to talk?"

Palmer rubbed at the stubble on his chin.

He had a curious look in his watery brown eyes. Ed wondered what Janet Murphy saw in him.

"What you want to know? Say, can we walk and talk. It's almost quittin' time, and I'd like to put this wheelbarrow back and get on home."

They fell in beside him as he crossed the street.

"Louis," Ed said. "Did Janet say anything to you last night about Violet Wertheim or her sister?"

Palmer stopped in the middle of the street and stared at Ed.

"Did Janet tell you that?"

"It doesn't matter who we heard it from, son, did she or didn't she?"

"So what if she did?" His eyes were narrowed in anger. "She's always talking 'bout how these rich bitches look down their noses at us who work here. That Violet Wertheim's the worst of the lot, too—always insulting Janet's cookin'. Hell, Janet's a damn fine cook."

Ed started walking slowly to give Palmer a hint that standing in the middle of the street wasn't a particularly good idea. When a car came around the corner and the driver honked at him, he finally moved on across, stopping again when he came abreast of Ed and Ernesto.

"When she told you this, what did you think?" Ernesto asked.

"What you mean, what'd I think?"

"What he means," Ed said. "Is did you think of doing something about it?"

Palmer looked away, and then down at his feet.

"What the hell can I do? What kinda question is that? Why you asking me?" As he glared at them, Ed noticed just how close set and porcine the man's eyes were. Again, he wondered what Janet Murphy saw in him.

"Just curious," Ed said. "No particular reason."

"Well, if you ain't got no more crazy questions, I gotta get this wheelbarrow back to the club and get home."

Without waiting for a response, he walked away. Ed waited until he was about half a block away and began following him.

"What are we doing?" Ernesto asked in a stage whisper.

"Just curious to see where he's going. I have a feeling he's hiding something."

They stopped half a block from the clubhouse and watched as Palmer pushed the wheelbarrow around the side of the building nearest the starter shack. A few moments later, he emerged from behind the building, walked to the parking lot, got into his fire engine red Chevy Silverado double cab pickup and with the engine roaring like a C-130 cargo plane drove off.

Ed shrugged. "I guess he was in a hurry to get home."

"You think he's involved in Violet's kidnapping, don't you?"

"Yeah, amigo, I do."

Ernesto shook his head.

"So, why aren't we following him? We might find Violet."

"No, I don't think so. He'd never have gotten her past the gate. I think Violet's here somewhere."

Ernesto shook his head again, and ran his hand through his hair.

"I don't get it," he said. "If he kidnapped her, and he's got her somewhere here, why's he driving off?"

Ed rubbed his chin. He noticed that he needed a shave.

"Good question. Could be he's got her all locked away somewhere, could be he's got someone helping him. After all, he has to do his job around the compound, so he can't watch her even when he's here."

"We gonna follow him anyway?"

"Well, I promised Sergeant Janzen I'd stay out of his way. If we go snooping around outside the community, he might find out and not be too pleased. So, I think I'll just share my little theory with him and see if he can look after Louis on the outside."

FOURTEEN

Ed decided to wait until Monday, to talk to Janzen. He woke up unsettled, the case was on his mind, and had, in fact, kept him from a good night's sleep on Saturday night, and kept him on edge all day Sunday. He woke up before sunup on Sunday, ate dry toast and coffee, and sat in his kitchen with a yellow notepad jotting down everything he knew about the situation. He didn't make it halfway down the first sheet.

At 10:00 he went across the street to his friend's house to compare notes. They ended up going to the golf course and playing a desultory 18 holes, during which time they spent more time talking about the case than paying attention to their game, resulting in them losing 10 balls between the two, including one shanked ball on number 13 that hit a tree a ricocheted down into the little valley with the pond and maintenance shed. They were both so preoccupied with finding and rescuing Violet they didn't even bother trying to find lost balls.

After golf, they went back to Ernesto's house where they grilled hamburgers and drank beer while continuing to discuss the case. Neither of them could come up with any useful ideas as to what they should do next, though both felt bad that they might have to let the police handle it.

Ed went home at 6:00 pm on Sunday, frustrated and no small bit tipsy—they'd consumed an entire case of Corona beer, and other than a couple of over-done burgers, eaten little.

He sat in his living room until well after 11:00, staring at the half page of notes on his legal pad, scratching his head, and cursing his inability to figure things out. Finally, just before midnight, he brushed his teeth and collapsed into bed. His sleep was troubled by dreams of Violet, held prisoner somewhere wondering if someone would come and save her, and his late wife, scolding him for failing to pick up after himself.

At 7:15 Monday morning, late for Ed, a man who was usually awake and at it by 6:30 every morning—a habit left over from his days in the military—he woke up. His head throbbed and his mouth felt like someone had stuffed unripe persimmons in it. He stood under a hot shower for twenty minutes to ease the headache, and brushed his teeth with baking soda to rid himself of the gunky feeling and odor. By the time he'd consumed a bowl of oatmeal and two cups of hot, black coffee, he almost felt normal.

Time to get down to business and solve the kidnapping. First, though, he had to get help with Louis Palmer.

At 9:00 he called police headquarters and asked if he could see him. Janzen told him he'd come to PVC, which was fine as far as Ed was concerned. He'd never liked driving in area traffic, and while Rockville wasn't as bad as downtown DC, it still drove him nuts the mindless, self-centered way that people drove; as if the vehicle they were driving was the only occupant of the roadway.

He was on his third, and hopefully final, cup of coffee when his doorbell rang. He put the cup, half-finished, on the coffee table and answered the door.

Carl Janzen, his suit looking like he'd slept in it, gray-brown stubble on his cheeks, and with dark lines around his blood shot eyes, stood on the front step. He hesitated, a querulous look on his face, when Ed opened the door and stepped aside.

Ed looked at his watch. It was 9:35. The sergeant had made good time from Rockville.

"Good morning, sergeant," he said. "I was just having coffee. Won't you come in and join me."

As he walked in, Janzen looked around the living room. He ambled toward the couch, stopped for a few seconds, then plopped down on the cushion nearest the door.

"Yeah, I'll have a cuppa joe." He fumbled around in his jacket pocket and removed his note pad and a black ballpoint pen. He put them on the coffee table. "I like mine black."

Ed went into the kitchen and got the half-filled container from his coffee maker on the kitchen counter and a ceramic mug from the counter, and brought them back into the living room. He filled the mug and handed it to Janzen, then refilled his own mug. He sat on the cushion at the end of the sofa opposite Janzen.

After taking a long drink, he put his cup down. "Any progress on finding Violet?" he asked.

Janzen blew on his coffee, made slurping sounds as he took a drink, and then put the cup down. He rubbed his eyes with the backs of his hands and then pinched the bridge of his fleshy nose.

"No, sorry to say, we've canvassed almost half the houses—haven't started on the condos yet—and have come up with bupkis."

"I really don't think she's in anyone's house," Ed said. "Or in any of the condo units either."

Janzen blinked his eyes. He rubbed the corner of his right eye with a knuckle.

"What makes you say that?"

"Have you met any of the other residents? Violet Wertheim is a . . . formidable woman. I seriously doubt there's a resident here who could overpower her, and this is a . . . well, let's just say that it would be difficult for someone to forcibly take someone into a house without a neighbor noticing."

"I've only met a few." Janzen chuckled. "But, the two cops I have doing the canvas have briefed me. You make a good point. I also checked with the security guards at both gates, and I've watched them work. It's unlikely someone would have been able to take her off the compound. So, where the hell could she be, and who could have taken her?"

For all his rumpled appearance, Janzen continued to impress Ed with the quality of his thinking. He'd come to the same conclusions himself. He wrestled internally for a few seconds, and then decided to take be more open with the man.

"I, uh, know I promised not to interfere with your investigation, sergeant," he said. "But, I did a little snooping of my own on Saturday, and I have a theory, but I've no way of confirming it."

Janzen picked up his notepad and pen and looked expectantly at Ed, who then filled him in on his conversations with Janet Murphy and Louis Palmer, and shared his suspicion that one or both of them might be involved in Violet's disappearance. Janzen scribbled away as he talked. When he'd finished, Janzen snapped the notebook shut and put it back on the table.

"I oughta ream you for freelancing," he said. "But, you've come up with the best lead yet. For what it's worth, I think you're right; one or both of these people are probably involved. I'll get a tail on 'em right away. Maybe they'll lead us to where the Wertheim woman's being held."

"There's just one problem," Ed said. "Janet lives here in the community. She has a unit in one of the condos. Louis, on the other hand, lives outside, I'm not sure where. But, neither of them would have been able to sneak Violet out, because even staff vehicles are checked when they leave—it's part of the fair treatment policy." As he spoke, another idea occurred to him. "And, given their duties, I'm beginning to think they have help."

"What makes you think that?"

"Janet's on duty at the community center all day until after supper and Louis is responsible for grounds keeping at the golf course as well as the rest of the community. I'm thinking they have to have someone keeping watch on Violet."

"Someone else on the staff?"

"Maybe, but it would have to be someone who isn't expected to be available to the community throughout the day, and I haven't been able to figure out who else on the staff would fit that description."

Ed could feel Janzen's eyes on him,

lancing through him like a laser, as the man inspected and analyzed him. He felt like he should say something, wanted to say something, but his years of working in a byzantine bureaucracy where the most trivial expression could, and often would, be twisted beyond comprehension, had taught him that sometimes the best thing to do was nothing. The best way he'd learned to have influence and power was to allow others the illusion that they had control. He sat quietly meeting Janzen's gaze, his craggy brown face as impassive as the granite slabs covering the Pentagon's walls.

Finally, Janzen seemed to have come to some inner decision. His expression changed, from probing to something approaching warmth; or as close to warmth as Ed imagined he was capable.

"You know, Ed . . . you mind if I call you Ed?" Ed shook his head. "You know, I think I was wrong about you."

"Wrong, in what way?"

"Usually when well-meaning civilians insert themselves into an investigation it's because they're trying to cover something up, and in most cases, even when they're not, they manage to screw things up. But, you, you've got a first class mind. Thinking back, you never promised you wouldn't snoop around. You just said you wouldn't get in my way. You're honest, but in a sneaky way. I like that. Plus, you've come up with a better lead than I had, and without access to my resources."

He took another sip of coffee.

"And, you make a damn good cup of coffee. So, here's the deal. You keep snooping around here in the community. These people are your neighbors, so you can get away with talking to them about things that if I ask about will just fuel gossip. In the meantime, I'll have my people start digging on the outside, starting with this Palmer guy, and do background checks on the staff here."

"I'll do what I can, sergeant."

"Call me Carl," Janzen said. "Just one condition, though. I don't want you going off and playing Magnum, PI on me. If you learn something, pass it to me and I'll handle it."

Ed shrugged and held his hands out, palms up.

"Really, ser-, Carl, I'm a 68-year-old retired civil servant. Do I look like the type to play hero?"

In fact, Ed was in excellent condition for his age. He worked out regularly, and still managed to practice taekwondo two or three times a month. Except for a slight bulging around the waist, he had very little fat on him. He'd estimated Janzen to be a few years south of fifty, although he looked Ed's age. But, Ed knew how to play the game.

Again, he hadn't lied. He hadn't promised Janzen that he wouldn't try to rescue Violet if he learned where she was being held.

He could also tell from the wry expression on the cop's face that Janzen was well aware of that.

Janzen confirmed it by standing, smiling, and saying, "Just take care, okay."

FIFTEEN

Less than five minutes after Janzen's departure Ed heard a rapping at his front door.

"It's not open, amigo, come on in," he said. He knew that it was Ernesto. He was the only person in the community who never rang doorbells.

Never one to enter a room quietly, Ernesto shoved the door open so hard it banged against the doorstop and caused a vase on the stand near the front to vibrate.

"So, what'd the cop have to say?" Ernesto asked, not breaking stride as he crossed the room, and headed for the kitchen.

Ed waited for him to return, which he shortly did, carrying a mug. He filled it with coffee and plopped down on the sofa next to Ed, looking at him over the rim of the mug as he drank noisily.

Watching him, and seeing the anticipation in his eyes, Ed decided to string him along—just for a few moments. Ernesto's brows wiggled and his eyes goggled over the rim of the mug. He began bouncing up and down on the sofa, threatening to send coffee slopping over the rim. Finally, Ed decided he'd had enough fun at his friend's expense.

"I explained our theory," he said. "And, he agreed with me."

"You mean he wasn't ticked off that we ignored his warning about sticking our noses into his investigation?"

"Considering that we found a lead he missed, he really didn't have anything to complain about." Ed went on to describe the deal he'd made with the detective.

"So, we're the inside guys, and he's the outside man?"

"Yeah, something like that," Ed said. "Now, let's map out our activities for the day."

"Sure. Hey, got anything to eat?"

"Eat? Man, it's 10:30; too late for breakfast and too early for lunch."

"Who said anything about breakfast or lunch? I'm talking 'bout my mid-morning snack."

Ernesto went on at length about the importance of eating small amounts throughout the day rather than just three big meals, until Ed started feeling hunger pangs. So, Ed gave in and made them salami sandwiches which they washed down with buttermilk. After slaking the Ernesto-induced appetite, they sat around the dining table and began strategizing.

It was decided that they would split up, with Ernesto keeping an eye on Janet Murphy, while Ed staked out the golf course to see what Louis Palmer was up to. They would keep in touch by mobile phone. Ed didn't bother telling Ernesto of his promise to keep Janzen in the loop.

"Before we do that, though," Ed said. "Let's check in on Rose and her niece."

They found the two women sitting on the patio, untouched cups of tea on a table between them. They were sitting quietly, their sad eyes not looking at anything in particular. Rose looked up as Ed and Ernesto came around the corner.

"Good morning, Ernesto, good morning, Ed," she said. Her eyes were sad, and her voice was without spirit. "Would you like to join us for tea?"

Peony looked up, nodded without speaking, and went back to staring at nothing.

"Hey, Rose, Peony," Ernesto said. "How you two holding up?"

"Good morning, ladies," Ed said.

Peony looked back at Ernesto with a scowl on her face.

"How are we holding up? Aunt Violet's still missing, we haven't heard anything more from whoever kidnapped her, and for all we know she could be dead by now. How do you think we're holding up?"

"Now, dear," Rose said. "No need to snap at Ernesto. He was just being polite."

"Hmph!" Peony said.

Rose looked at them and shrugged. The two men just smiled. "We're pretty confident we'll find Violet soon," Ed said. "I spoke to the police officer in charge of the investigation this morning, and he thinks we might have a suspect in our sights."

"Really," Peony said without looking up. "What is he going to do today to get her back? Who is the suspect?"

"Uh, well, it's a little early to start naming names, you understand. But, I feel like today will be our lucky day."

"Yeah, whatever."

Ed was miffed at the young woman's rudeness, but he also understood her frustration. So, instead of taking her to task, he just shrugged.

"Don't worry, Rose," he said. "We'll keep you posted. If you get a call from the kidnappers, call me as soon as you can— preferably before you call Sergeant Janzen, okay?"

"Sure, Ed, I certainly will."

Ed and Ernesto walked together a block, to the corner of Wisteria and Evergreen, before splitting up.

Palmer was reseeding the putting greens when Ed arrived, so he went inside the clubhouse and got a table near the window where he could watch him. He nursed a cup of coffee until it was so cold it had scum on the surface; for an hour and a half, Palmer carefully scraped away the grass on the practice putting surfaces, aerated the soil, and laid in squares of new sod with deep green grass, aligning them so carefully that from where Ed sat the seams were invisible.

At noon, Palmer stopped working and headed toward the clubhouse. Ed tensed, worried that the man might see him and suspect that he was being watched, but at the last minute, Palmer changed course and headed toward the shelter where golf carts were stored, a large structure consisting of a corrugated iron roof set atop four metal pylons. He reached into one of the carts and withdrew a metal box, which he opened and from it he took a sandwich and a thermos jug. He then sat in the cart and began eating his lunch.

As he watched Palmer tuck into his sandwich, Ed's stomach started growling. He glanced at the rank of vending machines just beyond the display of overpriced golf accessories. *He just started eating. He's not going anywhere for a few minutes.* Convinced by his inner voice, Ed took a quick look to confirm that Palmer hadn't moved—he hadn't; he was slouched down on the seat of the golf cart, biting absently at his sandwich and looking furtively from side to side as if he knew he was being watched. Fortunately, he didn't seem to think of the clubhouse as a vantage point from which his watchers might keep an eye on him. He never looked in that direction.

Ed went quickly to the vending machines. After fumbling around in his pockets for coins, he discovered that he only had enough for a Snickers™ Bar and a can of Barq™ Root Beer. He took his purchases back to his observation post. Palmer appeared not to have moved. Ed sat down and slowly ate his 'lunch' and continued to watch.

Palmer worried at his sandwich, and took occasional sips from the cap of his thermos, all the while looking all around like a man who knows he's being watched. At one point, he took his mobile phone from his overall pocket and had an animated—looked like a short, but heated argument to Ed—with whoever called him. With an angry motion, he terminated the call and started to put the phone back into his pocket. He hesitated. Then, he held the phone up and pushed the buttons. Holding the phone to his ear, he had another animated conversation, but this time, rather than looking angry, he looked nervous.

Ed would have given anything at that moment for one of those little parabolic antennas he'd seen advertised in the back of comic books when he was a kid; the kind that let you eavesdrop on distant conversations. If not that, it'd be nice, he thought, if he could read lips. Alas, he had neither, so he could only observe and speculate. He speculated that Palmer had received a call about Violet's kidnapping, a call that angered him, and then called someone else—probably his partner in crime—to pass along whatever it was that had upset him. *Nice speculation, Ed Lazenby, but nothing you can take to court. Hell, nothing you can even share with Carl Janzen without sounding like an eccentric old coot.* He found it amusing that he'd started thinking of the policeman as a person with a name rather than just an official title. There was something about the man, though, that Ed found interesting, and even a bit endearing. He had a first-rate mind. A useful trait for a policeman. But, he also had the ability to listen, process new and perhaps contradictory information, and then to make adjustments in his thinking to accommodate that new information. A trait that most people in Ed's experience lacked.

He hoped Ernesto had better luck watching Janet Murphy. In Ed's view, if she was involved in the kidnapping, she was definitely the weak link. He continued to hope that she wasn't. He hoped that her crime had been having a big mouth and sharing information with her scruffy boyfriend that should never have been shared.

After finishing his lunch, Palmer put the thermos and lunch box away and, still glancing around furtively, went back to work on the putting greens. He worked until 4:30, and then took the wheelbarrow and tools back to the cart shed. After looking all around, he went to his pickup, got in, and drove off in the direction of the main gate.

Ed followed on foot. It wasn't difficult keeping the pickup in sight. The speed limit within the community was 25 MPH, and Palmer kept well within it. The street from the golf course to the main entrance was straight, and Ed was able to see that, after a brief stop to have his pickup searched, Palmer exited onto Norbeck Road. Hoping that Janzen had surveillance in place to follow him outside the community, Ed picked up his pace and headed toward the community center.

He found Ernesto in the dining room, at a table near the front, with a full glass of iced tea at his elbow. He was reading the comics from the Sunday *Washington Post*, and casually keeping an eye on Janet Murphy, who was flitting back and forth between the two buffet lines, supervising her two assistants as they set up for dinner. The dining room was otherwise empty.

"How's it going?" he asked as he sat in the chair to Ernesto's right.

"Bor-r-ring," Ernesto said.

Before Ed could inquire further, Murphy

was at his right side, a weak smile on her face.

"Hi, Ed," she said. "It's too early for dinner, but can I get you something to drink?"

He looked up at her. Her face looked a bit pale and her expression was wary, but she still had her trademark smile.

"I'll have what Ernesto's having," he said.

She looked at Ernesto and frowned.

"He's been sitting there looking at that glass of tea for the past few hours, but if that's what you want, I'll be right back."

With a glance over her shoulder, still frowning, she went to the farthest line and filled a tumbler with tea, adding a slice of lime. She brought it back and put it at Ed's right side. He picked it up and took a sip. She smiled at him. He studied her over the rim of the glass as he took another sip. While she looked tired, and maybe a bit nervous, her expression wasn't too much different than it usually was just before a meal. He knew she must be thinking about the whispers, some loud enough to be heard at adjacent tables, that were the mainstay of meals in the dining room. While the food was edible, considering how much residents paid for the privilege of living at PVC, it left much to be desired. It reminded Ed of the meals he'd had as a young recruit when he went through basic training. Meant only to provide the energy to survive a hard day of training, they didn't appeal to a discriminating palate. While that might have been okay for a battalion of recruits who had no say in the matter, and who would never dare provoking the ire of their drill sergeants by complaining, it didn't appeal to the elderly residents of PVC. Try as he might, he couldn't see her as a kidnapper. *Maybe just the wishful thinking of old man.*

"This is good, Janet," he said. "And, you remembered to put in lime like I like it."

"I try to please my customers," she said. "Of course, you're about the only one to notice it."

She laughed and frowned again at Ernesto.

"Oh, I like it too, Janet," he said over the top of the comic page.

"Then, why aren't you drinking it?"

"I was just waiting for Ed. I hate to drink alone."

He gave her his thousand watt smile, showing off his brilliant white teeth. Picking up the glass, he took a long, noisy drink.

"You're terrible, you know that?" she said. Some of the color came back into her face, making her look almost beautiful.

No, I'm right. She can't be a kidnapper. But, that leaves the sixty-four dollar question; who is?

Ed quietly sipped his tea until she went back to her job across the room.

Keeping his voice low, aware that the

acoustics of the place made it possible for a normal conversation to be heard all the way across the room, he leaned in toward Ernesto.

"Did you see anything suspicious?"

"No, not a thing," Ernesto responded, also barely above a whisper. "She's been here all day."

"Did she make any phone calls?"

"Yeah, around noon, she went into the vestibule back there and made a quick call. I couldn't hear what she said, though."

So, Ed thought, while conversations in the dining room could be heard in the vestibule, apparently the reverse wasn't true. Must have something to do with the closeness of the space, he thought. But, that bit of news was interesting.

"Could you see her when she was on the phone? Did she seem upset or angry?"

"I didn't get a clear look. She seemed a bit nervous when she went back there, and she looked sad, I guess, when she came back. Why?"

Ed told him about the call he'd seen Palmer take.

"You think she called Palmer?"

"Yeah, the time fits, and he seemed to be yelling into his phone, which would explain her looking sad. I just wonder what it was all about."

Ernesto had put the comic page down and was playing with his glass, twisting it around and making little rings on the tablecloth from the condensation on it.

"Could have been a lovers' spat," he said. His brow wrinkled. "I can't for the life of me, though, understand what she sees in him. She's not that bad looking, and has a college degree, and he's just trailer trash."

Ed had been having the same thoughts, but he didn't want to go there. Ernesto had a habit of discussing peoples' sex lives, a habit Ed had never developed. Some things, he believed, should be off limits. Furthermore, Murphy's sex life wouldn't help them learn what had happened to Violet.

"You know," he said. "I think the only way to find out is to just ask her."

"Are you sure that's a good idea? I mean, if you ask her, she'll know we've been watching them."

True. But, if she wasn't involved in the kidnapping, it might just spook her into saying something that would prove it. If she was . . . he didn't want to think what that might cause. He was torn about it. His gut told him she wasn't involved, but his rational mind was pretty adamant that he'd be taking a big risk. He mentally flipped a coin. Heads I ask her, tails I don't, he thought. His mental coin landed on its edge. *Damn! Do I trust my gut instincts?* When he'd worked at the Pentagon he'd often faced situations like this. The numbers on a report didn't add up. Logic gave him one answer, but in his gut he knew the answer was something else entirely. In every case he could remember his gut had been right.

"I'm going to ask her," he said.

SIXTEEN

Ed left Ernesto sitting at the table. His friend's expression was unreadable. At first, he looked shocked and opened his mouth as if to protest, but the stern look on Ed's face caused him to snap his mouth shut. Then, he just nodded and went back to reading the comic page.

Murphy had just finished adjusting the stack of glasses near the tea and coffee urns when Ed approached. She looked up at him and smiled.

"You finish your tea already?"

"No, I still have a bit left," he said. "I, uh, I need to talk to you about an important matter."

"My, you look so serious when you say that." She smiled weakly. "Was there something wrong with the tea? It was freshly brewed this afternoon."

"The tea was fine, thanks. Look, can we go to your office? I'd like to speak in private."

She looked at him curiously, then shrugged and headed for the vestibule. Ed followed her to her office. Inside, nothing had changed since the last time except that she had a different binder open on her desk, this one a book of dessert recipes. It was opened and a recipe for key lime pie was marked. She glanced at the binder, and then at Ed. Her hand rested on the edge of the binder, lifting it as if to close it, then she let it lay open and sat. Ed closed the door and turned to face her.

"Okay," she said. "What's up?"

Ed decided to plunge right in.

"Did you talk to Louis Palmer on the phone today around noon?"

Her eyes went round in surprise. Red circles blossomed on her cheeks.

"Uh, why do you ask?"

"I don't like prying into anyone's personal . . . affairs," Ed said. "But, it's important."

"Well . . . yes, as a matter of fact, I did call Lou today."

"What time?"

"I don't recall exactly, around noon or so, I think. If it's important, I can check my phone and tell you the exact time."

"No, that won't be necessary. Now, this next question is gonna sound like prying, but it's even more important; what did you two talk about?"

The circles on her cheeks darkened. She closed her eyes.

"It's really, really important," he said. "If it's truly personal, you don't have to give me details."

Finally, she opened her eyes, but she didn't meet his gaze.

"If it was anyone else asking, I'd tell them it was none of their business. But, you're not like the others here, and I don't think you'd snoop into my private business without a good reason. I called him to see if he wanted to go to a movie tonight after supper. He said he had some important business to take care of and couldn't make it."

From what Ed had seen of Palmer's end of the conversation, he knew there was more than that.

"What else did you talk about?"

"Oh, yeah, after he said he couldn't make it, I mentioned that there'd been police officers around the community. Something to do with one of the residents missing or something."

Ah ha, he thought. That's more like it.

"How did he react to that?"

She looked puzzled. "That's strange, now that you mention it. He got real angry and told me to keep my mouth shut. I asked him why, and he got even angrier and hung up on me."

That gave Ed a sense of relief. Her body language, tone of voice and facial expressions all indicated she was being truthful, that she wasn't involved in Violet's abduction. He was worried at the same time, though. Apparently Janzen's discreet inquiries weren't so discreet after all.

"Where'd you hear about police being here and someone being missing?"

"Well, I saw those two young women going from door to door when I went on my run early this morning. My dad was a policeman, so I recognize a cop when I see one. As to one of the residents going missing, I think it was Candy Drummond who mentioned it in passing when I came to work this morning."

"Did she tell you who was missing?"

"Uh, no," she said. "In fact, she stopped talking as soon as she'd said it, like maybe she wasn't supposed to be telling me or something, you know. Is there some really missing? Who is it?"

"I'm sorry, I really can't tell you. And, I have to ask you not to speak of it to anyone else for the time being."

She pursed her lips. Her brows arched up toward her bangs.

"Oh, wait a minute! You and Ernesto were asking me about Violet on Saturday. Is *she* the one missing? Is that why the police are here?"

Ed held a hand up like a traffic cop.

"Like I said, this is something you shouldn't be talking about right now, to *anyone*."

She looked confused.

"Now, you're sounding like Lou. I-"

"Listen to me, Janet, this is important. It's crucial that you not talk about this." Especially that boyfriend of yours, he thought.

She made a lip zipping motion with her fingers.

"Okay, my lips are sealed," she said. "But, you'll tell me what's going on as soon as you can, right?"

Ed leaned across the desk and placed a hand on her shoulder. "Don't worry, you'll be among the first to know when things are settled."

He left her sitting there with an expression on her face that was a combination of confusion and relief. His next stop was Candice Drummond's office.

SEVENTEEN

Ed went back to the dining room.

"Come on, amigo," he said to Ernesto. "We've got to go see the nurse."

Ernesto gulped the rest of his tea, folded the paper he'd been reading and put it on the table.

"Why, you sick or something?"

"No, I'll tell you when we get there, come on."

"Wait, wait, wait, rush, rush, rush. Dang if it ain't just like the army, only instead of hurry up and wait, it's wait and hurry up," Ernesto grumbled as he followed Ed out of the dining room.

Drummond's office was in the administrative building, not too far from the executive offices and down the hall from Roland Vickers' office. There was an examination room between them, with access from both of their offices.

"Wait out here for me," he told Ernesto.

Ed walked in without knocking.

Drummond was seated behind her desk studying a large X-ray. She looked up, with a startled expression on her face, when Ed slammed the door open.

"Wha-"

"I need to talk to you, lady," Ed said.

Her face went rigid. "How dare you barge into my office and address me in that tone, Mr. Lazenby."

"No, *Ms.* Drummond. You eavesdropped on my conversation with Dr. Vickers last week, *and* despite hearing me ask him to keep it quiet and not inform the police, you called them."

She opened her mouth to protest, but the glare from Ed froze the protest in her throat. She swallowed hard and made an effort to regain a position of dominance.

"You were talking about a kidnapping, for heaven's sake. That has to be reported to the police."

Ed walked over and slammed his hands down on her desk. She scooted her chair back, cowering behind the X-ray which she held up like a shield.

"You put Violet's life at risk by calling the police. You should have talked to me or Dr. Vickers before doing that."

"B-but, the police are the ones who know how to deal with these kinds of situations."

Clutching his fists in frustration, Ed turned his back on her. He wanted to scream. She meant well, he knew that, but the road to a hot place is paved with good intentions like hers.

Finally, he took a deep breath and turned to face her. His look was cold, his voice even colder as he spoke.

"If anything happens to Violet," he said. "I'm holding you personally responsible."

"Wha-, are you threatening me?"

"No, I'm not threatening you, lady. That's a promise."

He turned again and stalked out. Ernesto took one look at the stormy expression on his face, and for once decided it best not to say anything.

EIGHTEEN

Ed was silent as they left the admin building, frowning deeply. He walked with his shoulders stiff and his fists clenched. Ernesto, able to remain silent only for short periods, could take it no longer.

"Okay, amigo, you want to tell me what went down between you and the nurse?"

Ed stopped and faced his friend. He told him about Drummond.

"Yeah, sort of figured that. So, why're you so pissed?"

"I . . . yeah, I guess I am making too much of it. It's just . . . she was so smug about the whole thing. She eavesdropped, and then took it upon herself to-"

"Hey, don't worry about it. We'll find Violet, you and me."

Ed's phone rang. He snatched it from his pocket. It was a 301 area code, but he didn't recognize the number.

"Ed Lazenby," he said.

"Ed, Carl Janzen." Ed could hear other voices in the background.

"Yeah, Carl, anything new?"

There was a rustling of papers.

"I think you're on to something with this Palmer character," Janzen said. His voice sounded a bit muffled, as if he was holding the phone in the crook of his shoulder. "I had a tail put on him. We pick him up whenever he leaves the compound, and stay on him. So far, he's done nothing all that suspicious, but I also had a background check on him, and I think we hit pay dirt. Turns out this jackass's sister is married to a local mobster wannabe, a goombah named Vincent Santini."

"Mobster? As in mafia?" Ed was stunned at that. That didn't sound good at all.

"No, nothing that fancy. Just local gangsters that do protection, loan sharking, penny ante stuff. He's low level muscle who apparently wants to move up to middle management; just the type to do something stupid like kidnapping an old lady."

"Why don't you pick him up and; what is it you guys do; sweat him?"

"Thought about doing that. I sent a unit to his last known address to pick him up for questioning, but he's gone A.W.O.L."

Now, that, Ed thought is *really* not good. He wondered if this gangster friend of Palmer's was somewhere on the grounds;

maybe watching them as they stumbled around looking for Violet, and laughing at their futile efforts. Or worse, torturing her because of their actions. *What have we done here? No, it's Drummond's fault. If she hadn't stuck her nose in and called the police.*

"So, what do we do now?" he asked.

Long silence. Ed's heart was pumping. Finally, Janzen spoke.

"Well, I had 'em put an APB out on this jerk. Don't worry, if he's anywhere in the DC area, we'll get him. Hell, one thing we're not short of around here is police forces. It's just a matter of time until he sticks his ugly mug up in public, and we'll take him down. You find out anything on your end?"

Ed didn't share Janzen's enthusiasm about the police forces' ability to find Santini. For one thing, they were looking in the wrong places.

"Well," he said. "I'm pretty convinced that Janet Murphy had nothing to do with Violet's disappearance. Palmer, on the other hand; I think he's in it up to his chin."

"You got any proof?"

"Janet told him about the police being here and, according to her, he flipped out. I know that's not enough to take to court, but it's suspicious."

"Yeah, it is. That and his connection with Santini makes him a good suspect in my book. We'll keep an eye on him out here. You keep him under watch there . . . just remember to be careful."

"Will do," Ed said. He rang off and turned to Ernesto. He looked crestfallen. "Amigo, we got a major problem."

NINETEEN

Ed explained the complication; the possible involvement of Vincent Santini in Violet's abduction. He didn't have to spell out the additional danger to her that caused.

"Holy shit," Ernesto said when he'd finished his explanation. "What we gonna do now, man?"

Ed looked up at the graying sky. "Not a lot we can do this late in the day, but hope Violet's okay wherever she is. I think we should go over and make sure Rose and Peony are okay. Maybe I'll order some takeout for us; Chinese sound good to you?"

"If it's food, it sounds good. My stomach's clawing for my belt buckle right now."

Rose and Peony agreed to Ed's suggestion about ordering food. He called the Panda Express situated a few miles away in

Rockville on Viers Mill Road and ordered Beijing beef, king pao chicken, Chinese pork spareribs, honey walnut shrimp, fried rice, white rice, and chow mein noodles. When he hung up, he explained that they would be sharing the dishes Chinese style.

"You seem to know a lot about this stuff," Peony said. "Why didn't you order in Chinese?"

"I only know a few words of Chinese," Ed replied. "And, the person taking my order was named Rosita, so she probably wouldn't have understood."

Peony's face turned red, and Ernesto laughed, which earned him a withering stare from the embarrassed young woman. Ed ignored their byplay and sat on the couch, where Rose poured him a cup of jasmine tea.

Normally fully made up and professionally coiffed, Rose had a wan look, her lipstick was smeared on the right side of her mouth, and tendrils of her blue hair draped over her ears. Her dress, a long-sleeved number that stopped at mid-thigh, was wrinkled at the waist, and one of the sleeves had a stain on it.

"How are you holding up, Rose?" Ed asked.

She swiped at the hair at her ears, but it flopped back, then she looked up at Ed. Her eyes glistened with unshed tears.

"I . . . oh, I don't know what to think. If anything happens to Violet, well . . . how I wish we'd never come up with that stupid idea."

She began quietly weeping. Ed put a hand on her shoulder. He could feel her body shaking.

"Don't worry, Rose. We're gonna find her. I promise you that."

She took the lace napkin from her lap and wiped her eyes, smiling up at him.

"I know you will, Ed. We're so lucky, Violet and I, to have friends like you and Ernesto."

The doorbell rang. Peony ran over and opened it to a young Hispanic guy holding a large box from which wafted aromas of spices and meat.

"I got an order for Ed Lazenby," the delivery guy said.

"You've got the right address," Peony said. "How much do we owe you?"

"That'll be forty-five dollars."

Peony turned and arched her eyebrows at Ed, who was already on his way to the door, opening his wallet as he walked. He extracted two twenties and three fives and handed them to the man in exchange for the box, which he passed to Peony. The man smiled expectantly at Ed.

"Keep the change," he said. "You mind setting this out on the dining table, Peony?"

"Gracias, senor," the delivery man said.

Without answering Ed, Peony spun on her heels and went into the dining room as Ed closed the door. Rose stood up and followed

Peony.

"Food's here guys," he said. "Let's eat."

"It does smell good, doesn't it?" Rose said as she arranged four plates, complete with forks and spoons around the table, followed by tea cups and glasses and a pot of tea in the center.

Peony put the entrees, rice and noodles in the center near the teapot and distributed napkins and the little packets containing wooden chopsticks, soy sauce, hot sauce, and orange sauce at everyone's place. Ed started to one side, but Rose insisted that he sit at the head of the table, with Ernesto to his right, Peony to his left, and her taking the hostess position at the end opposite Ed, but also nearest the kitchen. Ed marveled at how she could so quickly into the role of effortlessly playing hostess after looking so down just moments before.

They shared the main dishes around the table, each taking some of each. Ed added fried rice, while Ernesto took fried rice, white rice, and a large helping of the noodles. He smiled and shrugged when Peony frowned at him.

"Hey, I been doing a boring stakeout all day," he said. "Gotta replace all that energy I burned."

"What kind of energy do you burn sitting around on your ass?" Peony asked.

Rose reached over and slapped her playfully on the shoulder. "Now, Peony, young ladies don't use such language."

"Sorry, Aunt Rose." But, she didn't really sound sorry.

Ernesto laughed.

"I like a woman who speaks her mind," he said.

"Ernesto, stop encouraging her. You're worse than Violet." At the sound of her sister's name coming from her own mouth, Rose's face fell again.

"Come on, folks," Ed said. "You can't eat Chinese food with long faces." Using his chopsticks, he picked up a piece of chicken and dipped it into the hot sauce. "Now, eat up before it gets cold."

They fell to eating, Ernesto with noisy gusto, using a fork and spoon, Ed quietly with chopsticks as did Peony, and Rose, daintily, at first making an effort to emulate Ed and Peony, but after the food dropped off the third time, giving up and copying Ernesto with a fork and spoon. In a short time, there was little left but the greasy plastic containers the food had come in and about two cups of tea in the pot. Rose poured cups for Ed and Ernesto and dragooned Peony to join her in the task of cleaning the mess from the dining table and brewing a fresh pot of tea.

Ed and Ernesto went into the living room and sat on the sofa drinking their tea. Ed had just put his cup down when his phone rang.

He took it out and looked at the screen. It

was a 240 area code, somewhere in the local area, but it was a number he didn't recognize. Hoping it wouldn't be someone trying to sell him something he flipped it open and held it to his ear.

"Hello," he said.

"Is this Ed Lazenby?" A husky male voice boomed in his ear.

"Yeah," Ed replied. "Who is this?"

"It don't matter who it is. You just shut your trap and listen." Ed could hear banging and muffled voices. "Stop that racket; I'm tryna make a phone call here." The racket got louder. "Aw shit. I'll go outside where it's quiet. Hold on a minute, Lazenby." Ed heard the heavy sound of footsteps on a hard surface, a creaking sound, the thud of wood on wood, and the banging and muffled voices stopped. "Okay, where was we? Oh yeah; listen up Lazenby. I got the dame, and if you wanta see her alive and in one piece, you'll follow what I tell you. Got it?"

"Yeah, I got it," Ed said. "But, who the hell are you, and who is this dame you're talking about?"

He crossed his fingers that his transparent attempt to keep the caller on the line hadn't been seen through. And, then, he mentally kicked himself. It was *Rose's* phone that the young police computer technician had arranged to have remote monitoring of after a weekend of no calls.

"The dame I'm talking about is Violet

Wertheim, smart ass," the voice said.

Ed breathed a sigh of relief. The man didn't sound too smart. It had to be Vincent Santini, he thought, the mobster wannabe. Ed understood that designation now. It didn't make him any less dangerous—perhaps even more—but, it meant there was a chance to outsmart him.

"Okay, I'm listening."

The man made a harking sound and spit. The phone was so close to his face, Ed heard it clearly. *Stupid and ill-mannered to boot.* He also heard a strange background noise, muffled and indistinct, but also familiar, which was drowned out when the caller spoke.

"Okay, Lazenby, here's what you gonna do. You gonna get five hundred G's, you gonna put 'em in a plastic bag, see. Then you gonna take that bag to the Pineview Mall on Norbeck Road, and you gonna put it in the trash can outside the barber shop. You gonna do that at midnight tonight, and you ain't gonna have no cops nowhere near that mall. You got all that?"

Ed was tempted to say no, but thought better of it. He did, though, want to stall for time. There was something nagging at him in the back of his mind, and he needed time to think on it. He was sure, for reasons he could not even explain to himself, that it was important.

"Yeah," he said. "I got it, but I've also got a

problem. You're calling me instead of Violet's sister. That's just going to slow things down."

"Hey, you think I'm stupid or something. I know you called the cops, and I know they got this broad's sister's phone tapped. I also know you're close to these broads, so just get the money."

Well, that was close to confirming Palmer's involvement.

"Okay, sorry about that. We're not the ones who called the police."

"Yeah, I know that. That's why I didn't off the old broad. But, you better follow my instructions from here on out, get it?"

"Yes, I have it," Ed said. "There's one other problem, though. Since you're going through me, it means I have to consult with Rose, and I don't think she can get that much money together by midnight tonight. In fact, I *know* she can't. Can we have a couple of days?"

"What you think this is, Home Shopping Network or something? You trying to jerk me around?"

"No, no, not at all. But, you're asking for a large sum. We don't have that kind of money just lying around in cash. Rose will have to go to the bank, and she'll probably have to explain why she's withdrawing such a large amount." Ed wasn't even sure if Rose *could* withdraw such a large amount. "All that will take time."

The caller didn't respond. Again, Ed heard the muffled sounds, as if they were coming through some kind of curtain. He strained to hear, still thinking they were familiar, but unable to identify them. Finally, he heard raspy, nasal breathing in his ear.

"How much dough can you get by tonight?"

He looked around the room He knew that, after paying for the take-out, he had about twenty dollars left in his wallet. Ernesto might have forty or fifty in his. He could only guess how much money Peony might have in the small purse she'd put on the credenza in the corner of the living room, and he knew that Rose never carried cash. Violet always paid for meals in the dining room, and she never carried more than a hundred dollars in her purse. Of course, the kidnapper would already have access to that.

"We don't often have a lot of cash on hand here," he said. "Mostly we just use our credit cards, and all of mine are maxed out at the moment. If I had to guess, I'd say we can scrape up a hundred, maybe two hundred dollars."

That was answered by a loud snorting sound.

"Hell, that's not enough, not by a long shot!"

"I know that. That's why we need more time." Ed tried to keep all emotion out of his voice.

"Damn! Okay, I'll give you one more day. You got until tomorrow night. Five hundred grand in a plastic bag, in the trash can in front of the barber shop at Pineview. You got it?"

It wasn't what he wanted, but an extra day was better than nothing.

"Okay, I got it."

Sudden silence followed by a dial tone told him the caller had broken the connection. Now, all Ed had to do was find Violet, and he had just over 24 hours to do it.

TWENTY

"There's no way we can come up with five hundred thousand dollars by tomorrow night," Peony said. Her face was red and her expression was a mix of anger and anguish. "Hell, there's no way we could raise that much in the next six months."

Rose sat next to her niece on the couch clutching a handkerchief to her chest and looking bewildered.

"I knew we wouldn't be able to get it today, because the banks are already closed," Ed said. "But, I was kind of hoping you had access to your joint bank accounts, Rose."

Rose looked up with a pained expression.

"Well, I don't. Our bank account is in Violet's name. I guess you'd have to say it's really *her* bank account. I have a little trust fund in my own name—my mother left it to me when she died—but, it doesn't have *that* much money in it."

Ed breathed in and out in an effort to calm his nerves. Things were rapidly going from bad to worse. The clock was ticking and his options were dwindling.

"Maybe we could cut up some paper and put some real money on top of stacks like they do in the movies," Ernesto said. "Then, after we deliver it, we stake out the drop off point and follow the kidnapper to where he's holding Violet and rescue her."

Everyone turned and stared at him.

"You learn that working for the Post Office, Skippy?" Peony said.

The sarcasm stung him. Ernesto's face screwed up into a pout.

"You don't have to be so nasty about it," he said. "I was just trying to be helpful."

"If that's what you call help, we're in big trouble," she said.

Rose looked like she wanted to cry.

"Okay, okay, let's ease up," Ed said. "We're not helping Violet by attacking each other." He patted Rose's hand. "So, only Violet has access to the amount we need? Maybe we could let the kidnapper know, and use that to get him to go with her to the bank and-"

"Wouldn't do you any good," Peony said.

Three heads swiveled her way.

"Why not?" Ed asked.

"Uh, Aunt Rose, I'm sorry you have to

learn this under these circumstances, but that fortune Uncle Mortimer left Aunt Violet isn't exactly a . . . fortune."

"Not a . . . what on earth do you mean, Peony?"

"It's a long story, one my mother told me just before she died." Peony stood, hugging her arms to her chest. She walked around the coffee table and turned to face them. "Uncle Mortimer was, as you well know, Aunt Rose, something of an eccentric. He collected stamps and books, and did a lot of traveling. In his lifetime, he made millions, but he also spent it—all of it practically."

"B-but, I was there when they read he will. He left his entire estate to Violet."

"Yes, his entire *estate*. That means more than money. He left all his possessions to Violet. According to mom, that was about fifty thousand dollars and his physical assets, his stamp collections and his books, and I doubt if together they're worth more than twenty or thirty thousand."

Rose seemed to shrink into herself. Her pale face was ashen.

"Oh, my goodness," she said. "What are we going to do?"

"We're going to find Violet," Ed said. "We're going to rescue her."

"How, how?' she wailed. "We don't know where she is. We don't know who kidnapped her. We don't have the money to pay the ransom?"

Then a thought exploded in Ed's mind. Kidnappers went after people with the means to pay ransom. Why would anyone target Violet? Because they thought she had money. Where did they get that information?

"Has Violet ever talked about her inheritance other than Friday night when we were having dinner at the community center?"

"Uh, no. She sometimes talked about it here when it was just the two of us, but as far as I recall that's the first time she ever said anything in public."

And, Ed thought, Janet Murphy was nearby when she did. He took out his cell phone and hit number 4 on speed dial, the community center.

"Potomac Valley Community, community center," the perky voice of the duty operator announced in his ear.

"Yeah, this is Edward Lazenby. I need to talk to Ms. Murphy in the dining room."

"Please hold." He heard a few notes of the recorded music from the system, and then Janet Murphy's voice came through. "Janet Murphy here, how may I help you?"

"Janet, Ed Lazenby. When we spoke the other day, and I asked you about you talking to your boyfriend, Louis Palmer . . . did you mention to him that Violet Wertheim talked about inheriting a lot of money from her uncle?"

"Uh, yes I did as a matter of fact," she

said. "You know, I was talking about how some of these rich old folks like to lord it over we poor menials. Why?"

"Just checking something. Thanks for your help, Janet. You're good people."

"Thank you-" He cut the connection before she could finish.

"It's Louis Palmer, probably with help from his brother-in-law, Vincent Santini. Janet mentioned Violet's inheritance to Palmer that night."

"We sort of knew that all along," Ernesto said. "How is that gonna help us now?"

"I'm thinking on that," Ed said. "Just give me a few moments to mull it over."

"Oh my goodness, this has just been a week of bad news," Rose said. "What else could go wrong?"

"Aunt Rose," Peony said. "There's one more thing I think you need to know."

Rose looked confused.

"W-what else could you add to what's already been a terrible week?"

"Well, for starters . . . and, this is according to my mom, mind you . . . Aunt Violet is only your half-sister."

"What! You're . . . we have the same parents. Violet, me, and your mother, Daisy."

Peony made a face.

"Grandma and her obsession with flower names," she said. "My mother had it. That's why I'm stuck with the dumb name, Peony. Anyway, dear Aunt Rose, you and Aunt Violet only share the same mother. You had different fathers."

"How do you . . . how did Daisy know this?"

"She said when she was eight, she was looking through the family Bible and she noticed Violet's birthdate. It just happened to be three months after grandma and grandpa's wedding, so she got curious and starting checking. When she was twelve, she found an old shoebox behind some trunks in the attic. In it were letters to grandma. You remember your father; he'd never go in the attic. He was afraid of ladders. Anyway, mom read those letters. They were from grandma's first love—who was also Aunt Violet's father."

Rose's lips quivered.

"Y-you, don't m-mean . . . it can't be-"

"It is, er, was. That's why grandpa never got along with him, and why he left everything to Violet when he died. Aunt Violet's father was Great Uncle Mortimer."

Rose's mouth opened in a circle. Her eyes crossed. She crumpled to the floor in a dead faint.

TWENTY-ONE

After reviving Rose, and listening to her apologies for having 'the vapors' for nearly an hour, Ed and Ernesto returned to their respective homes.

For Ed it was a restless night. He lay in bed for a while, reading in an effort to clear his mind, but was unable to clear his mind or pay attention to what he was reading. After an hour, he put the book on the nightstand, turned out the light and lay back. But, that didn't help either. He tossed and turned for hours, finally drifting into a fitful sleep around one in the morning.

His dreams were all over the place. Images of his wife, Olivia, from their courtship when she was just graduating from college and considering a career as a teacher, the years when they tried vainly to start a family, the day the doctor diagnosed the cancer that finally took her away from him, merged with images of Violet Wertheim; Violet sitting in the dining room complaining about the food, the weather, and just about everything else under the sun, Violet kneeling in her backyard tending her flowers while Ed, Ernesto and Rose sat on the patio sipping tea. Among the other images, though, were the troubling images of Violet in a dimly lit space, bound and gagged, with a large dark figure looming over her.

He woke up at 5:30, drenched in sweat despite the chill in the room, only vague fragments of his dreams still in his head, but with a determination to get Violet back home safely and see her abductors behind bars.

After showering and shaving, he took care in choosing his wardrobe for the day. His hands moved on autopilot as they selected a pair of black cargo pants, black cotton shirt, black socks, and his black Timberland hiking boots. He admired himself in the full length mirror on his bathroom door. *Well, don't you like a special commando?* He then went into his kitchen and made himself a breakfast of four slices of bacon, an egg over medium, two hash brown patties from his freezer, and four biscuits from a roll of ready-mades he'd bought at Giant. The remaining six biscuits he wrapped in plastic and put in the crisper box of his fridge for later.

His body cleansed and fortified for the day, Ed had one more chore to perform before setting out. He called Carl Janzen for an update on the detective's progress in locating Palmer's accomplice Vincent Santini.

"We're still coming up empty," Janzen said. "It's like the guy got zapped up by aliens or something. No one in his neighborhood's seen him since last Saturday morning. You come up with anything on your end?"

"No. I'm still convinced our groundskeeper, Louis Palmer is involved, but I haven't been able to catch him at anything."

"Okay, but listen, Ed, I'm serious about this. Don't put yourself in danger trying to take him on by yourself. Just observe and report."

Ed looked down at the black legs of his cargo pants and smiled.

"Of course, Carl, I'll just keep an eye open, and if I see or hear anything I'll call you right away."

"You see that you do," Janzen said just as Ed pulled the phone away from his ear and snapped it shut.

At 6:45, he left his house and headed across the community picnic grounds toward the golf course. As he passed Ernesto's house, his friend came running out onto his patio.

"Hey, Ed, where you heading?"

"I've got a little business at the golf course."

"You gonna talk to Palmer?"

"Thought I might."

"Need me to come along?"

"No, you go and keep an eye on Rose and Peony. I'll take care of this."

He kept walking, knowing Ernesto wouldn't let any harm come to the two women.

He was just entering the long curving drive to the clubhouse when he saw Palmer's pickup pull into the employee parking lot. Palmer got out and was starting to the cargo compartment when he looked up and saw Ed approaching. He turned and walked back to the front of the vehicle. He had a querulous frown on his face. He was unshaven, and looked like he'd slept as poorly as Ed had.

"Morning, Mr. Lazenby," he said. "You playin' golf today? Where's your clubs?"

"I'm not here to play golf, Louis. In fact, I came here to talk to you."

Palmer's bloodshot eyes narrowed to slits.

"Why you want to talk to me? You got some work needs doin' at your place? I can't get to it this week. Maybe next week, unless it's an emergency."

Ed thought about taking a subtle approach, feeling Palmer out, but as he stood there looking at the man's bloodshot eyes and smelling the rank odor of stale booze on his breath, he decided to go for the jugular.

"No, I don't need any work done. What I do need, though, is for you to tell me where you and your friend Vincent are keeping Violet Wertheim."

Palmer's eyes widened a fraction, for just a heartbeat, enough to tell Ed he'd hit the right button. But, the man recovered quickly.

"I don't know what you're talkin' about." He balled his fists and leaned forward. His face turned red.

Ed stood his ground. He and Palmer were about the same height, but the man was at least thirty years younger and had a good fifteen pounds on Ed.

"I think you know exactly what I'm talking about. I think Janet Murphy repeated something she'd overheard, and you saw a chance to make some quick money and strike back at the snobby rich folks who you think are always looking down their noses at you. How'm I doing?"

Raising his fists to shoulder level, Palmer made gurgling sounds.

"You just like the rest of the people here. You get the cops to come snoopin' 'round because some rich old bitch wanders off or something. Well, you got it wrong. So, get out of my face and leave me alone."

He dropped his arms, whirled around and stalked off toward the cart shed. Ed walked away, sneaking a quick peek into the back of the pickup as he did. In the back, he saw a large cardboard box containing four paper bags, two of them with grease stains. That must have been what Palmer was about to remove from the back, he thought. He thought about staking the parking lot out to watch for Palmer retrieving the box and the following him, but then realized that by confronting him like he had, he'd made that very difficult if not impossible to do.

So, he decided to go to the Wertheim house where he could have some quiet time to consider his next move—hopefully.

TWENTY-TWO

Ernesto, Rose, and Peony were sitting on the patio, taking advantage of a warm October morning when Ed arrived.

Rose reached for an empty cup from the table near her chair and filled it with tea.

"Come and join us for a cup of tea," she said, holding the cup up for Ed.

"Don't mind if I do," he said.

He took the cup and took a sip before sitting on the chair between Rose and Peony.

They sat, sipping their tea in silence, looking at nothing in particular; a pose that was familiar to the three older members of this little tableau, but a source of frustration to Peony, younger and unfamiliar with their ritual.

"So, what are we going to do, sit here and gaze at the clouds and wait for divine inspiration?" The frustration she felt gave her words extra velocity as they pierced the companionable silence.

Rose frowned. Ernesto looked worried. Ed's expression, as he met her gaze, was passive. His face was like a carved mahogany bust, absolutely unmoving, until he spoke, "No, Peony," he said; his deep, resonant voice quiet but firm. "We can't do anything right now because we don't know where Violet is."

"Why don't the police do something? Why can't they find her?"

Ernesto snorted.

"That guy Janzen seems smart enough," he said. "But, most of the cops I know can't find their noses with both hands. They wasted all that time going from house to house, as if any resident here had the strength to kidnap a woman like Violet."

"So, where should they be looking?" There was challenge in Peony's voice.

Ernesto looked down at his size twelve Nike sneakers.

"Uh, I don't know." He turned to Ed. "You got any ideas, amigo?"

Ed had been turning that question over in his mind; over and over; but without coming to anything remotely resembling an answer. He was the leader of their little group, by default though, so he had to convey the appearance of being on top of the situation. He was reminded of a passage in a *Star Trek* novel he'd read some years earlier, where James T. Kirk, captain of the *Enterprise* was explaining leadership to a younger member of his crew. He could never remember it literally, but the gist stuck in his mind; a good leader convinces everyone around him that he's in command of the situation, but he does not try to convince himself. He knows that he neither knows nor controls everything, and is therefore prepared to respond when things, as they inevitably will, go wrong.

"I haven't figured out yet where the kidnappers are holding her," he said. "But, there are two things I feel pretty sure of.

He held up a finger.

"One, I'm pretty sure Louis Palmer is somehow involved in this.

Up went the second finger.

"And, two, because of the vehicle searches at the gate, I'm convinced she's being held somewhere within the community. Problem is, there are so many outbuildings, she could be in any one of them, or even be moved among them under cover of darkness."

"They wouldn't necessarily have to drive her out," Ernesto said. "This place isn't entirely fenced in."

"I thought about that. You're right of course. There's only the brick walls at the entrances, there more for show than security, since they only extend a hundred yards to either side of the gate; and you have the chain link fence near the golf course; but, that's there mainly to keep anyone from wandering from the woods onto the course and getting beaned by a stray golf ball. Problem is; Violet's a handful at the best of times. She wouldn't go willingly, and I can't see someone, even someone as hefty as Palmer, carrying her through the woods like a sack of flour."

"You got a point, but how do we figure out where she is?"

"You could grab Palmer and beat it out of him," Peony suggested.

"As tempting as that might sound," Ed said. "It probably wouldn't work. Besides, it would be illegal."

"So what," Peony snapped. "He deserves it if he kidnapped Aunt Violet. I'm sure they had to rough her up to take her. What's good for the goose is good for the gander, I say."

Ed looked at her. A sudden light went on in his brain. He smiled broadly.

"Peony, you're a smart girl," he said. "You just told me where Violet's being held. I could kick myself for not having realized it earlier."

"Y-you know where Violet is?" she said, a look of utter confusion on her face. "How did I tell you?"

"Just now when you said the word goose. When the kidnapper called me I heard strange noises in the background. I couldn't make them out clearly, but I thought they were familiar. It's been bugging me since." He felt like kicking himself on the one hand for taking so long to make the connection, but on the other hand, felt good that he finally had. "The noise I heard, well, noises in fact, were geese honking. But, there was also another noise, and that I think is what threw me off. It wasn't a honking sound like geese make, it was more a kind of squawk. And, it just so happens I know what bird makes that sound, and I know where the two sounds are made together. I *know* where Violet's being held captive."

TWENTY-THREE

"Are you sure she's being held in that storage building off the thirteenth green?" Ernesto asked.

"As sure as I see your slightly overweight body sitting across from me," Ed said with a tone of conviction. "Great blue herons are territorial birds, and unlike the geese that move about from feeding ground to feeding ground, tend to stay close to their nests. The only place I've seen them here is that pond near number thirteen—a nesting pair, too. It's also a favorite feeding ground of the geese."

Peony had an anxious look on her face. Her hand shook as she lifted her cup to drink tea, spilling some on the table. Red-faced, she put the cup down and leaned forward.

"So, now you're going to call the police, right?"

"No," Ed said. "I'm pretty sure they have Violet there, and I'm also sure that if we called the police, they'd come in force and that would alert the kidnappers. There's no telling what they might do if they saw a squad of armed police closing in on them."

She looked shocked.

"You're not just going to sit here and do nothing. That's my aunt, and . . . you can't just leave her like that."

Ed patted her forearm.

"I didn't say I was planning to do nothing."

Ernesto smiled broadly, like a kid on Christmas morning. He began a tattoo on his thighs with his large hands.

"Okay, now I know why you dressed like a commando today," he said. "We're going on a rescue mission."

"You've *got* to be kidding," Peony said. "No insult intended, but you two are a little long in the tooth to be going up against a possibly armed criminal, aren't you?"

Ernesto sat back, a stunned look on his face. Ed had to stifle a laugh.

"I'll have you know," Ernesto said. "I was a postman for thirty years. I've faced dogs, snow storms, and carried a heavy mailbag like it was a small grocery bag. I'm in *good* shape, I'll have you know. And, Ed here was in the army. He's almost as good as I am."

"I'm not sure about that," Ed said. "But, I

do take offense at your ageism. We might be advanced in years, but we're not helpless."

"Oh yeah, and just what do you think you two *youngsters* can do?"

"Now, Peony dear," Rose said. "Ed and Ernesto are our friends, and we don't speak to our friends in that way."

Now it was Peony's turn to look offended. She turned and glared at her aunt.

"You're going to sit here and let these two-"

"That's enough, Peony." Rose's voice was icy. "We're going to let Ed handle this."

Peony looked down at her hands which were clasped and held in her lap. When she looked up at Ed, there were tears in her eyes.

"I . . . I'm sorry. I'm just so worried about Aunt Violet."

"I understand, Peony," Ed said. "I'm worried too. But, I think there's a way to deal with it. Just let Ernesto and I handle it."

She nodded, but there was still an apprehensive look on her face.

"Hey, kid, if Ed tells you we can handle it, believe him. He's got the brain and I have the brawn. We'll get your aunt back," Ernesto said. "And, that's a promise."

"Okay," Ed said. "You two take it easy. Ernesto and I are going to my place to make plans."

Ernesto rose and followed Ed around the house and up Wisteria to Ed's house. Ed went into the kitchen and started making a pot of coffee.

"I could use something a bit stronger than coffee right now," Ernesto said.

"Not until this is done," Ed said. "We need to have our wits about us. Have a seat in the living room; I'll be in as soon as the coffee's ready."

Fifteen minutes later, Ed walked into the living room carrying the coffee pot and two large mugs. He put everything on the coffee table and went to the credenza in the corner from which he took a yellow legal pad and two number two pencils. When he came back to the sofa Ernesto had already filled the two mugs.

"Okay, captain," Ernesto said. "We do the mission brief now?"

Ed ignored his friend and took a sip of coffee. He put the cup down and took one of the pencils and began drawing lines on the first sheet of the pad. He started with two parallel lines down the left side of the page. Next to that he drew another line, broken in two places. He labeled the first two lines, 'Georgia Ave.,' and the two blank spaces in the third line he labeled, 'Gate 1,' and 'Gate 2.' On the right side of the page he drew two wavy parallel lines much closer together than the lines on the left. These he labeled 'Service road.' To the immediate right of these lines, at the top of the page, he drew an arrow, writing an 'N' at the point of the arrow. He then began drawing in squares and rectangles between the parallel lines, starring with a large rectangle opposite 'Gate 1' labeled 'Community Center,' and small lines to represent the interior streets and major pathways. A medium-sized square north of the Community Center was labeled 'Golf Clubhouse.' He then roughly drew in the course itself, until he had all eighteen holes roughly sketched out. East of the hole he labeled '13' he drew a rough oval and a small square, and then made a lot of squiggles and curved lines from them to the Service road.

"Hey," Ernesto said. "That's a pretty good map of PVC. They teach you to do that in the army?"

Ignoring the question, Ed held the pencil over the square near the thirteenth hole. "This is where I think they have Violet," he said. "I think this Santini guy is keeping watch over Violet there, and Palmer is here." He moved the pencil over the clubhouse. "Keeping watch in case the police Janzen has canvassing the community start moving that way."

"Aren't they sort of boxed in there?"

"Not really." Ed shook his head and pointed to the Service road. "There's a fence along this road, but it only stretches from one end of the golf course to the other. It's open south of the course, and while carrying someone as heavy as Violet through those woods to the road won't be easy, it could be done, especially if two people were doing it."

"So, you think that if Palmer spots the cops moving in that direction, he hot foots it down and helps his accomplice move her?"

"That's what I'd do."

Ernesto shrugged and took a drink of coffee. "Ugh, I sure could use something stronger—okay, I know, keep our wits about us and all that shit. So, how do we play this?"

Ed drew an 'X' next to the storage hut, and then a circle adjacent to the clubhouse.

"I'm figuring Palmer's gonna find an excuse to work late today, and stay near the clubhouse to act as lookout. So, I want you to hang out near there and try to keep an eye on him. Try to not let him see you."

"And, what're you gonna be doing?"

He pointed at the squiggly shapes representing trees on the right side near the bottom of the sheet.

"I plan to go into the woods about where the golf course fence starts and work my way to the storage building," he said. "I don't think they'll be expecting anyone to come from that direction."

"Then you're gonna swoop in, surprise the bad guy and rescue Violet."

Unsmiling, Ed nodded.

"Something like that."

"Okay, dude; when do we start?"

"Just before dark; maybe five or so, you should be at the golf club. It'll take me a while to make my way through the woods.

It'll be dark by the time I get there."

Ernesto raised his cup.

"Ours not to reason why, ours but to do or die," he said.

"The proper quote is, 'ours but to do *and* die, amigo," Ed said. "But, I have no plans to die tonight."

He raised his cup and clinked it against Ernesto's.

TWENTY-FOUR

Ed and Ernesto had a final meeting at 5:15, and Ed watched his friend head off in the direction of the golf course. Once he was out of sight, Ed took a last look at his outfit, took a deep breath and took off in a brisk walk east toward the edge of the community. He crossed the tennis courts, walked past the art building and into the beginning of the forest, a sparse stand of evergreens, oak, maple and birch that ran a hundred meters to the community boundary. The sun was low, reflecting off the red, yellow, orange and brown of the fading fall foliage. When he reached the edge, in sight of the service road that ran the length of the east side of the community, he turned north. He'd only gone a few meters when the forest got thicker. The dead leaves underfoot making crunching sounds, a counterpoint to the tweeting of birds and the chirping of insects, dwindling slightly as the temperature dropped.

As the brush and trees thickened, Ed

found the going slower. He also began to sweat despite the lowering temperature, and not just from the exertion. He was nervous. His mouth felt dry. He was reminded of his time in the army, near the end of the Vietnam War, when he'd been sent to Vietnam right after advanced training, assigned to one of the last American units there posted in areas overrun at night by the Viet Cong. He'd felt the same way when his platoon was assigned to night patrol—like he could feel someone hiding in the bush taking aim at his back. It didn't help that the deeper he went into the forest the darker it got, with the low sun casting long, dark shadows over everything.

The sun was completely down by the time he reached the beginning of the golf course fence. He estimated from there that the shack was another four hundred yards north and one-fifty west. In the dark, with overhanging tree branches giving him only brief patches of sky, it would be tough to navigate. So, he decided to stay in sight of the fence for the northward leg of his journey, and then make his way west through the woods to the shack, hoping he didn't stumble into the pond in the dark.

He stopped and took a deep breath. Shaking himself to clear his mind, he started out again, counting his paces and watching the fence out of the corner of his eyes, never getting too close, but not so far away either. The trees didn't grow all the way to the fence, probably cut back to make maintenance of the fence easier, making it easier to travel, and with fewer trees the ground was more solid and easier to walk on.

Just when he'd estimated he'd gone the four hundred yards, he saw a dark shape outside the fence on the service road. He walked closer, and saw that it was a dark, late model sedan. *Must belong to Palmer's accomplice. Just as I thought; they had an escape route planned.* When he walked closer, he could see that a section of the fence had been cut away; just wide enough for a man to squeeze through. *Wonder why they didn't just take her away from the start. Oh well, lucky for us they didn't.*

Ed put his back to the fence and started walking forward. The spacing of trees and brush made it impossible for him to walk in a straight line, but whenever he came to an obstacle, he stopped, turned sharply to the right or left, walked forward until the obstacle was cleared, and then sharply turned back in the desired direction. He'd done this five or six times when he heard the honking of several geese, sounding as if it came from his right front. He angled generally in the direction of the sound and walked slowly forward.

The woods ended suddenly. One minute he was pushing his way through the dense undergrowth and dodging low-hanging branches, and the next he was standing in the far rough of the golf course. The mid-thigh high saw grass of the rough was like an immaculately maintained fairway after the experience of the woods. He stopped a moment to catch his breath, then looked around to get his bearings. A loud honking, and the 'awk, awk, awk' of the blue heron drew his attention to his right. He was about a hundred feet south of the storage building, which was a dark shape against the short grass and earth around it. The pond, at a slightly lower elevation, was out of his line of sight.

He stepped back into the shadow of a small oak tree, watching for movement in the vicinity of the storage building. Nothing moved. The only sounds he heard were the rasping of his breath, the gentle whisper of a breeze through the withering leaves of the hardwood trees, and the call of the geese and heron to his front.

It was time to commit. Ed knew this. He rarely went into anything with misgivings, because his analytical mind and career experience had taught him to assess the positives and negatives of any situation before execution, so that he had a good idea of the eventual outcome before beginning anything. This, though, was an entirely different kettle of extremely smelly fish. He hadn't been in any kind of physical altercation, other than wrestling with the plastic wrappers on products, for over three decades. Sure, he exercised regularly, and did his taekwondo exercises—he was extremely dangerous to the one-eighth-inch boards he smashed with the edge of his hand—but, exercising and demolishing unresisting wooding slats, he well knew, is not the same as dealing with a human adversary, and one that was likely to be armed.

He walked as he thought, and by the time he'd convinced himself that he was ready to 'do this,' he was a few feet from the corner of the storage building; close enough now to hear the sound of muffled voices and things being moved around from its interior.

Slowly, ever so slowly, he made his way around the structure until he was at the door. Up close, he notices that the building was one of those metal prefabs set on a poured concrete base, which protruded out an inch all the way around.

He put his ear to the thin wall beside the door. The noises, still somewhat muffled, were intelligible.

"Shut up and settle down, you old battleax," a male voice said.

"Hmph ung gnd und huhr ungbgn uhr nung," from a slightly higher pitched voice, which Ed assumed to be Violet speaking through some kind of gag.

This was followed by scraping and scuffling.

"Stop that, you dumb broad. Quit kicking

stuff at me."

The muffled voice responded again.

"Oh, screw you. I'm gonna go outside and leave you before I whap you over the head with something."

Footsteps on the metal floor could be heard approaching. Ed flattened himself against the side of the building.

The door swung open, throwing a warped rectangle of orange light across the dirt and grass. Inside that rectangle of light was a large, dark shadow that grew larger as its owner exited the structure. In the light cast from inside the storage shed, Ed saw a pear-shaped man of about forty with thin brown hair pasted to his round head, balding in front and making a lame effort to conceal it with an ineffective comb over, wide, rounded shoulders, and a Santa Claus-like belly that hung over his belt, dressed in a cheap, off-the-rack, rumpled blue suit, a food-stained white shirt, open at the throat, revealing a tuft of dark chest hair, and scuffed brown shoes. The man's left hand was clenched against his fleshy thighs and the right hand was making an effort to rearrange his comb over. His fleshy, florid face was a study in frustration.

He stepped from the building. Then, he turned to look back inside.

"You're nothing but trouble, lady. I'll be happy when they deliver the ransom, so we can get rid of you." Out of the corner of his porcine, brown eyes, he saw Ed standing there. "Who the hell are you?"

TWENTY-FIVE

Ed's breath caught in his throat. While the man standing there glaring at him looked fat and out of shape, he had a good twenty or thirty pounds on Ed. For a second, both men stood frozen in place, looking at each other.

Then, Ed charged at him.

Lowering his right shoulder, he shoved off the wall, and ran at the man like a football lineman, catching him in the chest, just below his sternum. The big man was turning as Ed hit him, so the blow caught him off balance, and sent him tumbling backwards, his hands flying upwards.

"Oof!" the fat man said as he landed on his back. His left hand went to the spot where Ed's shoulder had connected with his chest. The right was held up in front of his face. He seemed to be struggling to catch his breath.

As he started to push himself upright, Ed put a foot on his chest and pushed him back down.

"Just stay where you are, friend," he said. "Or I might have to really hurt you."

"Ur urig by ched, I cad brth."

Ignoring his mumbling, Ed pressed his foot down harder. The fat man's face turned dark, almost purple in the light from the shed.

"Is Violet okay?" Ed asked. "If you've hurt her, I'm going to bust you up good."

The man on the ground pursed his lips, blowing out, and then strained to pull air in. He moved his hands to Ed's foot, grasping and trying to lift it from his chest.

"You want me to lift my foot off your chest?"

The man lifted his head and bobbed it down toward his chest and up again, a pleading look in his eyes.

Ed lifted his foot. "You stay put. If you try anything, I'll put my foot somewhere it'll hurt even worse." He glanced down at the man's exposed crotch.

The man gasped, pulling air into his lungs. Finally, he looked up. Tears spilled down his face, into his ears.

"Okay, I ain't movin', just . . . don't put your foot on my . . . chest anymore, okay? I . . . got . . . asthma. Cuttin' off my . . . air like that . . . could kill me." He clutched at his chest, breathing with difficulty.

Ed had worked with an asthma sufferer at the Pentagon for a couple of years, and had seen similar symptoms when breathing was restricted. He knelt and did a quick pat down. The fat man had no obvious weapons. *Good grief. An asthmatic kidnapper who doesn't even have a nail file as a weapon.*

"Okay," he said. "I want you to get up real slow. You make one false move and I'll bust you good."

"Yeah, *gasp*, yeah, okay." The fat man started slowly pushing himself to a sitting position.

"What's your name?" Ed asked.

"None of your damn business."

Ed stepped forward and lifted his right foot, aiming it at the man's crotch.

"Okay, okay," the fat man said, leaning forward to cover his exposed midsection. "Vincent, Vincent Santini. What's it to you?"

"Just confirming what I already suspected. You're working with Louis Palmer, aren't you?"

A flicker of Santini's eyebrows and the way he looked away told Ed he'd got it right.

"And," Ed went on. "You parked your car over on the service road." Another flicker; and Santini looked up at him, his eyes wide. "What happened, you find you didn't have the strength to carry Violet through the woods to your car? I imagine she refused to walk, knowing her."

Santini looked like the air was slowly seeping out of his overweight body. His lips curled down in a sneer.

"Damned old bag ain't been nothin' but trouble," he said. "Kicked me in the shin twice when Lou and me was getting' her over here. Almost kicked me in the nuts, too."

Ed laughed. "Yeah, Violet can be a handful. Okay, stand up, but do it slow. We're gonna get Violet and walk out of here. I wouldn't try running or anything, either. You don't look like you can run too fast or too far, and if you try, I'm gonna be pissed, and I *will* kick you in the nuts."

Santini covered his crotch again.

"All right, no need to get violent." With some effort he heaved his body to a standing position.

Ed stepped aside.

"After you," he said, pointing at the door.

Santini stepped into the shed. Ed followed, keeping back so the man couldn't turn on him.

Violet, her eyes blazing and her hair in a mess, sat on a folding camp stool. Her hands were secured behind her and silver duct tape covered her mouth. Tools and equipment were scattered about. The place looked like it had been hit by a hurricane. As they entered, Violet began murmuring and dipping her head up and down.

"Take the tape off her mouth," Ed said.

Santini grasped the end of the tape near

her left ear and ripped it off.

"Ouch," Violet cried. "That hurt, you fat bastard. Ed, what took you so damn long to get here? I've got to go pee, and this fat fool won't take me outside."

"Last time I took you outside, you tried to kick me," Santini protested.

"I get loose, that's not all I'm going to do, you pig."

"Untie her hands," Ed said.

Santini looked pleadingly at him.

"Do I have to? She can walk with her hands taped."

'Gr-r-r, get this tape off my hands, you moron," Violet nearly shrieked.

"You see? This old broad's dangerous."

"Just untie her," Ed said. "Violet, we're taking Mr. Santini here to the police, so please don't assault him when he unties you."

She glared up at the fat man.

"Wel-l-l," she said.

"Come on, Violet," Ed said. "Please, just this once, be reasonable."

"Okay, I won't kick him."

"There, now untie her."

Edging around her, Santini clumsily knelt and began pulling the tape off her wrists. The tape came off with a sizzling sound. When her hands were free, Violet began massaging her wrists, which were red from the tight restriction of the tape. As Santini started to stand, she swung her right fist around and popped him on the end of his fleshy nose.

"Ow-w-w," he yelled as he fell back grabbing for his nose, which was spewing bright red blood. He ended up on his butt, looking up at Ed as he held his hands over his injured nose.

"Violet," Ed said. "You promised."

"I said I wouldn't *kick* him." She batted her eyes innocently.

"Okay, Santini, you'll live. Get up and let's go."

Still holding his nose, Santini looked up and smiled.

"I don't think so," he said.

Rose's eyes went round like saucers, and her mouth dropped open. "Oh, no," she said.

"What?" Ed asked

"Don't make any sudden moves," Louis Palmer's voice said from behind Ed. "Unless you want your brains spattered all over the place."

TWENTY-SIX

Ed resisted the urge to spin around quickly. He turned slowly and deliberately. Louis Palmer, still wearing his handyman's overalls and holding a three-foot length of metal pipe in his meaty right hand, filled the doorway.

"Damn, Lou," Santini said. "You got here just in time. This jamoke was about to haul me off to the cops."

"He ain't takin' nobody nowhere," Palmer said. "He's gonna be food for the fish, is what he is."

Ed held his hands shoulder high. He stared levelly at Palmer.

"You better think about what you're doing, Louis," he said. "You can't get away with this."

Palmer and Santini laughed.

"What'd I tell you, Vinnie? Ain't this old dude a hoot. You know, *Mister* Lazenby, I'm gonna really enjoy doing you." He glared at Violet. "And, as for you, you old prune, soon's that dipshit sister of yours comes through with the ransom money, you gonna take a long walk off a short pier too."

Violet made a squeaking sound.

"Hey, wait, Lou," Santini said. "We ain't said nothin' 'bout offin' nobody; just gettin' the ransom money."

Palmer's expression darkened. In those eyes Ed saw no mercy, nothing.

"What's the matter, Vinnie? I thought you was some kinda gangster. Ain't you got the balls for it?"

"It ain't that, Lou. It's just, when killin' ain't necessary-"

"Oh, shut up," Palmer said. "I don't what my sister ever seen in you. You ain't got no balls at all. They seen our faces, man. We *gotta* do 'em."

The reluctance on the fat man's face was apparent. While he might be a crook, he wasn't a killer. Palmer, on the other hand, had a look that Ed had seen in some of his platoon mates in Vietnam; he was a man who would enjoy killing someone. If he could somehow drive a wedge between them he and Violet might stand a chance.

"Don't listen to him, Vinnie," he said. "If

you get arrested for kidnapping Violet, and believe me, you will, you'll go to jail for a long time, but if you kill us, you're going to be behind bars for the rest of your natural life. You're lucky Maryland abolished the death penalty in 2013, or you'd be facing a date with a needle."

The fat man's face went from reddish to pale.

"I don't think you'd do too well in prison, Vinnie," he continued. "You let us go, and I'll put in a good word with the police."

"Shut up, Lazenby," Palmer shouted. "Don't listen to him, Vinnie. We kill these two and we're home free. Ain't nobody else knows us. We can get the money and get the hell out of the area."

"I . . . I don't know, Lou. I ain't never killed nobody."

"Shit, ain't nothin' to it. It's just like killin' a deer, or squashin' a roach. So, less'n you want to go to jail when that old bat identifies you to the cops . . ."

"Y-yeah, I guess you got a point." He frowned at Violet. "Actually, this bitch ain't done nothin' but give me a hard time since we snatched her. I reckon if I gotta start killin' she's as good a first one as any."

Palmer laughed harshly. "Now, that's what I'm talkin' about. Okay, Lazenby, turn around and get down on your knees."

The one thing Ed had no intention of doing. He had to force Palmer to come closer to him.

"If you're going to kill me, Palmer, you'll have to do it while you look me in the eyes— or, don't you have the guts for that?"

For a brief moment, no more than the blink of an eye, Ed saw hesitation in Palmer's expression. He hadn't expected his intended victim to face him down. Ed moved slowly into the fighting position his Korean instructor had taught him when he studied taekwondo, his feet about shoulder width apart, the left foot a few inches in front enabling him to kick with his dominant right foot, and with his hands near his waist with his fingers curled inward in preparation for making fists. He kept his eyes mainly on Palmer's eyes, knowing eye movement would be a better indicator of his intentions than movement of his hands, but also watched Santini, who was now standing, though still holding a hand over his bleeding nose.

Palmer remained in the doorway, waving the pipe across his body, glaring at Ed.

"You think I can't, old man? I can. I'm gonna bash your head in." Ed sensed hesitation in his voice.

"Well, what're you waiting for, big man?" he said. "Bring it on."

He knew he was taking a calculated risk baiting Palmer, but he wanted to get him off balance and keep him that way.

Palmer edged forward one step, raising the pipe to shoulder level. He made a growling sound deep in his throat. Ed tensed, ready to block the pipe. He sensed Santini moving toward him.

"I'm gonna bust your fuckin' head," Palmer roared, raising the pipe over his head.

Ed brought his left hand up, making a fist of his right.

"Ar-r-rgh! Aiy-yee!"

The sound just outside the doorway caused Palmer to pause with the pipe near his ear. Santini, Ed noticed peripherally, stopped in mid-move. Just as Palmer started to turn to investigate the source of the scream, a large figure dressed in brown sprang through the door, and Ernesto wrapped his muscular arms around Palmer's chest and shoved him forward.

Ed did a half turn to the right, raising his right fist. Santini began moving again. Violet stuck her foot between his legs, causing him to pitch forward. Ed's fist connected with the point of his chin, snapping his head back. His eyes rolled back in their sockets, and plunged forward. His head made a thunk sound as it hit the floor, unmoving.

Ernesto and Palmer were grappling with each other on the floor, but Ernesto had a few pounds weight on the younger man, and had him pinned face down. He began pounding his meaty fists into Palmer's head, neck and shoulders. The hand holding the pipe was crammed beneath his body, and with his free hand, Palmer was trying to block Ernesto's blows.

Ed took a quick look at Santini. Satisfied that he was out for the count, he rushed over and grabbed the thumb and pinkie finger of Palmer's free hand, and spread them apart.

"Ow," Palmer screamed.

Ernesto raised up, brought his fist back to his ear and slammed it forward into Palmer's temple.

Palmer grunted and went limp. Ernesto raised his fist to hit him again, but Ed grabbed his hand.

"He's out cold, Ernesto," he said. "Find something to tie him up."

"The duct tape they used on me is over in that corner," Violet said, pointing at a large roll of tape on the floor in the corner.

Ed scooted over and grabbed the tape. Quickly, they wound tape around Palmer's ankles and then pulled his arms behind his back and bound them as well. They were just finishing up with Santini, who was beginning to come around, when they heard a commotion outside the shed.

"You in the shed," a loud, command voice shouted. "You're surrounded. Come out with your hands up."

Ernesto sat back and smiled at Ed.

"The cavalry's arrived—late as usual."

"Is that you, Sergeant Janzen?" Ed called.

"Yeah, Ed, are you okay in there?"

"We are, and the bad guys have been neutralized. You can come in."

Janzen came to the door. His eyes went round when he saw the two taped up bodies on the floor. Two cops, wearing tactical gear and carrying automatic rifles crowded up beside him.

"Okay, boys," Janzen said. "Back up. The situation's been contained." He looked at Ed, his brows arched upwards. "You two did this?"

Ed smiled. "We had a little help from Violet."

Violet was sitting on the camp chair, a glum look on her face.

"I should've kicked that fat bastard in the balls instead of just tripping him," she said. She scowled at Janzen. "I need to get out of here. I've got to pee real bad."

TWENTY-SEVEN

At noon the next day, Janzen, a scowl on his face, sat across the table from Ed and Ernesto in the dining room of the community center. Violet sat to his right. Rose and Peony were to his left.

Ed was dressed in a pair of blue slacks and a black and blue plaid shirt. Ernesto wore his brown cargo pants with a Washington Nationals sweat shirt. Violet and Rose wore identical dresses, Violet's in green and Rose's in blue, with scoop necks and sleeves ending at mid-forearm. Rose had a pink hair clip in her blue hair, and Violet had given her scarlet curls another treatment of henna, turning them the color of a fire hydrant. Peony wore blue cargo pants similar to Ernesto's, but displaying a more pleasing shape, and topped them with a black shirt a size too large. She'd put on eye shadow which gave her a Gothic appearance that Ed actually thought somewhat attractive.

Janzen wore a gray suit that looked as if it had been taken crumpled from a laundry hamper rather than from a rack in his closet. He'd shaved, but his eyes were still red-tinged.

He fixed Ed and Ernesto with a glare as soon as they were seated at a table near the entrance.

"You two took a big risk going after those thugs by yourselves," he said. "You could've gotten yourselves or Ms. Wertheim here killed."

"The only weapon they had was that piece of pipe," Ernesto said.

"Yeah, but you didn't know that. I oughta arrest you two for interfering with an official police investigation."

"Hey, you can't do that," Peony said. "If your commando cops had come in with all their guns and bullhorns and shit, *they* could have gotten Aunt Violet hurt." Despite her words, Ed noticed a surprising tenderness in her voice.

Janzen's cheeks puffed out and turned pink.

"Now, Peony dear," Violet said. "The sergeant was just doing his job." She reached over and patted his hand.

"Thank you, Ms. Wertheim," he said.

"Oh, call me Violet."

"By the way," Ed said. "How'd you know

where we were?"

Peony blushed and looked down at the table.

"Peony called him," Rose said.

Ed looked at her.

"Why'd you do that?"

"I called and told her to do it," Ernesto said. "I was watching Palmer, and when I saw him heading toward the shed, I thought we might need a little backup, so I called the house and told Peony to call Sergeant Janzen and tell him where we were. Turns out we didn't really need him, but it saved you and me having to march them two back to the clubhouse."

"Yeah, I guess we would have had to call them then anyway." Ed smiled at Janzen. "Sorry I didn't call you, but-"

Janzen did the traffic cop thing with his hand.

"Forget it. Things worked out. My bosses were a little put out when I explained what happened last night. They were undecided whether you two should get medals for heroism or a night in the tank. In the end, since no one but the two perps got hurt, they decided to forget it. All's well that ends well."

Janet Murphy walked over and stood next to Janzen.

"Hi, folks," she said. She spoke to the table at large, but only had eyes for Janzen. "We have a special for lunch today. To celebrate Violet's safe return, you won't have to go through the buffet line. I'll have the staff bring your food. What would you like to drink?"

She wrote down their drink orders, still keeping her eyes on Janzen who didn't seem to notice her attention.

She looked at Violet with an expression Ed couldn't quite figure out. Violet looked back at her with her usual disdainful air.

"Yes, Janet dear," she said. "What is it."

"Uh, Violet, I . . . wanted to apologize for what Lou did to you."

"No need to apologize dear," Violet said. "It wasn't your fault."

In fact, during the walk to the community center, Violet had fulminated at length about how the whole thing was Murphy's fault for telling her trailer park trash boyfriend what she'd overheard. Ed had reminded her that she, Violet, had to share some of the blame for talking about such sensitive family business in a public place, after which, she relented and said she wouldn't blame Murphy for what happened—at least, not to her face.

Murphy seemed surprised that Violet wasn't being her usual acerbic self, but she quickly regained her composure.

"I thought you'd like to know, too, that Dr. Vickers somehow found money in the budget, and as of this morning, we have a new cook here in the dining room. I can now concentrate on planning meals instead of having to cook them."

This news got a big smile from Violet who gave Ed a 'See, I told you my plan would work' look.

"That's nice to hear, Janet," she said. "I've always said they were working you far too hard."

Murphy took the new Violet in, a look of near-disbelief on her face. Violet's tablemates, excluding Janzen who didn't know her well, shared skeptical looks.

"Well," Murphy said. "I'll get those drinks now. Your food will be here in a few minutes."

After she'd walked away to fetch their drinks, Janzen leaned over and stage-whispered to Ed, "Don't we get a choice in the food too?" he asked.

"The menu's a bit limited." Ed shrugged. "I'm sure she'll do right by us."

"She'll certainly do right by Sergeant Janzen," Peony said. There was a slight tension in her voice. "The way she was ogling him, I thought she was going to hop into his lap."

Janzen glanced at Peony without turning to face her directly. "Really? She was checking me out? Is she married?" His cheeks were now flame red.

"Oh, come on," Peony said. "She was staring so hard, you had to have felt it. And, for your information; no she's not married, but she was shacking with Louis Palmer."

Janzen pursed his lips. His cheeks turned

pinkish.

"Oh. In that case, it might not be a good idea for me to ask her out." He turned his head and winked at Ed and Ernesto.

"Should you even be thinking such a thing? A married man like you?" Peony's brows were raised.

"I'm not married," Janzen said. "Never have been."

Peony smiled. "Oh, I see. Well, enjoy your lunch."

Violet and Rose exchanged smiles. Ernesto looked from one of them to the other, looking puzzled. He turned to Ed. "What's that all about?"

"Don't worry about it, amigo," Ed said. "I'll explain it later."

Murphy brought their drinks. Her two assistants wheeled their food to the table on one of the rolling plate carts. Murphy fussed with setting the plates, spending a bit extra placing Janzen's plate just right, and finding an excuse to rub against his shoulder as he did so. Janzen's cheeks were now red, and he kept his gaze focused on his food, while Peony glared at Murphy. The Wertheim sisters smiled benevolently. Ernesto opened his mouth to say something, but Ed kicked him under the table, and shook his head. Poor Janzen had enough problems coming his way, Ed thought; he certainly didn't need Ernesto adding to his misery by asking an embarrassing question, or saying something out of turn.

Finally, frustrated at her inability to get the cop's attention, Murphy left them, but not before casting a withering glare at Peony who she'd correctly assessed as her competition for Janzen's attention. Aware now of the silent competition between the two young women, Janzen wisely focused all his attention on his food, but he had a satisfied smile on his face.

Violet Wertheim looked down at the withered green peas, slimy potato circles, and dried pork chops on her plate. She picked at them with her fork; took a small bite of potato. Then, she looked at Ed, a sly smile spreading across her face.

"Ed, dear," she said. "Would you pass the salt . . . please?"

Note from the author

There will be more stories about Ed Lazenby and his friends. Up till now, the protagonists in my stories have been around fifty years of age or younger. When I began writing *Butterfly Effect*, Ed was in his late fifties. Lately, though, I've been lecturing at the Osher Lifelong Learning Institute (OLLI) of Johns Hopkins University (JHU). OLLI is an adult continuing education program, and the average age of students is 67 to 68. I've been impressed with the spirit, mental and physical, of my students, so to honor them, I decided to age my protagonist. Some of the OLLI classes I've been lectured have been at satellite JHU campuses in the Washington, DC area that are located in retirement communities. I've been amazed at the variety of activities and amenities, including golf courses, in these communities, so I decided to make fictional Potomac Valley Community (PVC) the main setting for the Ed Lazenby mystery series.

Ed and his buddy, Ernesto, will be the main characters in this series (and, just in case anyone has noticed, I gave them first names starting with the same letter for a reason that will be explained in a future story), interacting with other community residents and staff, as well as townies like police sergeant Carl Janzen as the plot of a story dictates. In the course of writing this story, I developed a strong liking for Violet and Rose Wertheim—Violet in particular—so look for them in future stories as well. These characters are all figments of my imagination, but their archetypes can be found in the communities I've visited over the past two years.

I'm calling this new series the Ed Lazenby Mystery Series, but in truth I'm not sure how it should be classified. I suppose it really doesn't matter in the end, as long as readers like it. If (hope, hope, hint, hint) you do like it, please leave a review on Amazon, Goodreads, or your blog (if you have one). It's through reviews that indie books get discovered by other readers, so help an indie author out by spreading the word.

Other books by this author:

Al Pennyback mysteries
Color Me Dead
Memorial to the Dead
Deadline
Dead, White, and Blue
A Good Day to Die
The Day the Music Died
Die, Sinner
Deadly Intentions
Death by Design
Till Death Do Us Part
Deadly Dose
Dead Man's Cove
Dead Men Don't Answer
Deadly Paradise
Kiss of Death
Death in White Satin
Death and Taxis
Deadbeat
A Deadly Wind Blows
Death Wish
Deadly Vendetta
A Time to Kill, A Time to Die

The Buffalo Soldier series:

Buffalo Soldier: Trial by Fire
Buffalo Soldier: Homecoming
Buffalo Soldier: Incident at Cactus Junction
Buffalo Soldier: Peacekeepers
Buffalo Soldier: Renegade
Buffalo Soldier: Escort Duty
Buffalo Soldier: Battle at Dead Man's Gulch
Buffalo Soldier: Yosemite
Buffalo Soldier: Comanchero
Buffalo Soldier: Range War
Buffalo Soldier: Mob Justice

Ed Lazenby mysteries
Butterfly Effect

Other fiction
Angel on His Shoulder
She's No Angel
Child of the Flame
Pip's Revenge
Wallace in Underland
Further Adventures of Wallace in Underland
Dead Letter and Other Tales
The White Dragons
The Dragon's Lair
Dragon Slayer
The Last Gunfighters
The Culling

Frontier Justice: Bass Reeves, Deputy
    U.S. Marshal
Angel on His Shoulder-Revised Edition
Battle at the Galactic Junkyard
Mountain Man

Nonfiction

Things I Learned from My Grandmother About
    Leadership and Life
Taking Charge: Effective Leadership for the
    Twenty-first Century
Grab the Brass ring
African Places: A Photographic Journey
    Through Zimbabwe and southern Africa
A Portrait of Africa
There's Always a Plan B
In the Line of Fire: American Diplomats in
    the Trenches

Children's books

The Yak and the Yeti
Samantha and the Bully
Molly Learns to Share
Where is Teddy?
Catie and Mister Hop-Hop

About the Author

Charles Ray has been writing fiction since his teens. He won a Sunday school magazine writing contest when he was thirteen, and having his byline on a short story published in a national publication forever hooked him on writing. During his time in the army (1962-1982) he often moonlighted as a newspaper or magazine journalist, and was the editorial cartoonist for the Spring Lake (NC) News, a weekly newspaper, during the 1970s. In addition to his writing, he was an artist/cartoonist and photographer for a number of publications, including Ebony, Eagle and Swan, and Essence, and had a monthly cartoon feature and did several covers for Buffalo, a now-defunct magazine that was dedicated to showcasing the contributions of African-Americans to the country's military history.

After retiring from the army, he joined the U.S. Foreign Service, and served as a diplomat in posts in Asia and Africa until his retirement in 2012. He has worked and traveled throughout the world (Antarctica is the only continent he hasn't visited), and now, as a full time writer, continues to globetrot looking for interesting things to write about, draw, or take pictures of.

A native of Texas, he now calls Maryland

home. For more on his writing and other projects, check one of the following Web sites:

http://charlesaray.blogspot.com
http://charlieray45.wordpress.com
http://www.twitter.com/charlieray45
http://www.facebook.com/charlieray45
http://www.flickr.com/photos/charlesray45/
http://www.viewbug.com/member/charlesray

Author's photograph by Denise Ray-Wickersham